D1540231

'Don't worry.' Laura stood up, holding a now sleeping infant. 'There's a baby's car seat in the ambulance store room. We'll borrow that for the day and Megan can sleep in it.'

A ray of hope shone from Jason's smile. 'Shall…shall I hold it, then, while you go and find the seat thing?'

Laura bit back a wry smile as she handed Jason his daughter. 'She's not an "it", Jase. Her name is Megan.'

The bob of the Adam's apple on Jason's neck gave away his nervous swallow, but, to his credit, he looked quite calm as he regarded the tiny, peaceful face. He cleared his throat and spoke very softly.

'Hi, Megan…I'm Jase.' He cleared his throat again. 'Your…um…dad, I guess.'

Laura hurried towards the store room, swallowing rather hard herself to clear the unexpected prickle of tears.

EMERGENCY RESPONSE
Doctors… Police... Fire... Ambulance...

Police officers and paramedics, nurses and fire officers: meet the dedicated men and women of the emergency services.

Every day is packed with drama as they race to help others. But while they're saving lives... they're finding love!

THE FIREFIGHTER'S BABY

BY
ALISON ROBERTS

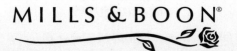

MILLS & BOON®

The Fire fighter Baby it de 1st Book & the
Emergeny At InGLewood iz 2nd, the
both go together:

With thanks to the guys at Sockburn Fire Station,
Christchurch, New Zealand, for their help in researching
this story. Especially, Dave, Paul, Ray and Mark
on Brown Watch.

*First published in Great Britain 2004
Large Print edition 2005
Harlequin Mills & Boon Limited,
Eton House, 18-24 Paradise Road,
Richmond, Surrey TW9 1SR*

© Alison Roberts 2004

ISBN 0 263 18467 6

*Set in Times Roman 16½ on 17½ pt.
17-0705-50346*

*Printed and bound in Great Britain
by Antony Rowe Ltd, Chippenham, Wiltshire*

CHAPTER ONE

'IT'S OK, sweetheart. Everything's going to be OK.'

For a split second, paramedic Laura Green envied the girl whose head she was holding. How crazy was that? She tightened her grip to ensure she was providing stability for the potential neck injury of the nineteen-year-old. The girl had been travelling home at the end of a night shift in a rest home. She had rounded a corner too quickly, run smack into the back of a heavy, slow-moving street sweeper and now lay trapped and terrified inside the wreckage of her car.

'Keep very still, Courtney,' Laura reminded her patient. 'Don't try and move your head.'

She could understand why the girl wanted to turn towards the owner of that voice. The words were so comforting, the tone completely sincere, and while the endearment was automatic it had the effect of creating an instant and powerful connection. And it was that connection that Laura envied.

She had never had anyone so totally focussed on her well-being. So committed to protecting and helping her. Not that she would want to experience it in a professional setting like this, of course. Courtney had a fractured right elbow and left femur and goodness only knew what condition her lower legs were in, trapped and hidden beneath the crushed front section of her small car.

A whimper escaped the injured girl as the car rocked slightly. The fireman now crouching beside the open driver's door leaned in far enough to be seen without causing another attempt to move.

'It's OK,' he repeated. His smile was reassuring. 'The car's moving a little because we're putting some blocks in to stabilise things. Then we're going to get you out of here.'

'It hurts…my leg hurts.'

Laura twisted her own head to peer through the shattered glass of a back window. Her partner, Tim, was approaching with a cervical collar in his hand and she could see the other supplies he had set out on a blanket beside the wreck. Some of the tension evaporated as Laura took a deep breath. They could get moving now. Get their patient's neck protected, get some oxygen on, an intravenous line in place and some pain relief on board.

'And…and I'm *scared*!'

'I know you are, sweetheart. But hang in there. You're doing just fine.'

Tim leaned past the bulky figure of the fireman assigned to patient communication. Laura adjusted her grip to allow the collar room to slip behind the girl's neck. The fireman straightened and stepped back to allow Tim more room to manoeuvre, but his action elicited a forlorn cry from the accident victim.

'Don't go. Oh, please, don't go!'

'I'm right here.' A heavy glove was stripped off and Laura frowned as she saw the fireman catch the fingers of the hand stretched towards him.

'I'm Jason,' the fireman introduced himself. 'What's your name?'

'C-Courtney.'

The neck collar was secured. Tim slipped the elastic of an oxygen mask over the patient's head and squeezed the metal band at the top of the mask to make it a snug fit over her nose.

'Pleased to meet you, Courtney.' Jason's grin made his teeth gleam in the powerful artificial lights now set up to illuminate the rescue scene. 'How're you doing?'

'N-not so good.' The response was broken by a frightened sob.

Tim hung his stethoscope back around his neck. 'Chest's still clear,' he told Laura. 'Equal air entry.'

Laura nodded, but she was reaching into the pocket of her coat with one hand.

'Put some gloves on, Jase.' She passed them over the barrier the front seat created.

'Sure.' The fireman was smiling at Courtney again. 'I'm in trouble now,' he confided. 'Laura's going to tell me off later for forgetting my gloves.'

The sound that now came from the injured girl sounded like a cross between a groan and a giggle.

'I'd rather not cannulate this arm.'

'No.' Laura agreed with Tim's decision. 'Not with that elbow injury.' There was no way of knowing how well the blood vessels were still functioning below an injury like that.

'Have we got access through the passenger door?'

'Not yet.'

'Is that what you need?' Jason's quick shift of attention revealed that his focus wasn't entirely on the girl he was comforting. A quick glance over his shoulder made him nod with satisfaction. 'The gear's all ready to go. We can start cutting wherever you need it.'

'C-cutting?'

'The car, sweetheart—not *you.*' Jason seemed to fill most of the remaining space in the crushed car as he leaned even closer. 'We're getting you out of here, remember?'

Courtney clung to him with her uninjured hand. 'It hurts,' she sobbed. 'Get me out *now.*'

'I can reach the other arm,' Laura told Tim. 'Pass me the gear. You should be able to maintain alignment from where you are now that she's in a collar.'

'I can hold her neck,' Jason offered.

'That would be great. I'd like to get a blood pressure done.'

'No!' Courtney refused to release the hand she was holding.

'Keep still, Courtney,' Laura instructed. She squeezed the top half of her body through the gap between the front seats. This job would be so much easier if she were *skinny*. Even a few kilos off would help. The flash of annoyance increased a second later when she had to push her dislodged spectacles back into place. Small irritations that would normally not distract her at all from the job in hand. Was it simply her close proximity to Jason Halliday that was making her aware of them now?

'Laura needs this hand, love,' Jason was saying. 'Once she gets a little needle in, she can give you something to help that pain.'

'No! I *hate* needles. And my hand feels funny. Just get me *out*!'

'What kind of funny?' Laura queried.

'It's got pins and needles.'

Laura caught Tim's glance. With a symptom that suggested an even stronger likelihood of a spinal injury, they were going to have to manage this extrication with particular care.

'It might help if you keep holding her hand, Jase.' Laura tightened the tourniquet and swabbed an area she could reach easily on Courtney's left forearm. 'This shouldn't take long.'

Jason obliged. He also placed his other arm gently on Courtney's shoulder, ready to stop any struggle if necessary. Then he tried to distract the terrified teenager.

'You're lucky you've got our Laura here,' he told her. 'Do you know, I've been working with her for six months now and I haven't heard a single complaint from any of her patients?'

'You haven't met many of my patients,' Laura muttered.

'She's a fireman?' Courtney's surprise indicated that the distraction was working.

'Nah. She's not tall enough to be a fire officer. Our station is a base for both fire and ambulance. Just one of each. We're on the outskirts of town in Inglewood.'

'That's where *I* live.'

'Cool. You'll have to drop in and visit us. Mrs Mack makes the world's best scones.'

'All done,' Laura announced. 'I'm going to give you some morphine now, Courtney. You're not allergic to any drugs that you know of, are you?'

'No.' The distraction Jason had been providing was still working a treat. 'Who's Mrs Mack?'

'She looks after our station. It's kind of a long story.'

'I'm just giving you something to make sure the morphine doesn't make you feel sick,

Courtney.' Laura injected the dose of meta-clopramide.

'Is she your wife?'

Jason chuckled and Laura found herself smiling wryly as she snapped off the top of a glass ampoule to add morphine to the saline another syringe already contained. Jason Halliday married? Tied down to single choice from amongst the model-like creatures that entered his social orbit? That *would* be the day!

'Mrs Mack is at least sixty,' Jason informed Courtney. 'She's Scottish and she's as tough as an old boot. She lives next door to the station and kind of adopted us. We're in an old house that got converted and...'

And Courtney didn't appear to be listening any longer. Her eyelids fluttered shut as the morphine took effect and her distress was obviously diminishing despite the increase in noise and activity of the rescue workers outside the vehicle. Another helmeted figure appeared between Jason and Tim, who was still maintaining Courtney's spinal alignment.

'How do you want to get her out?'

'Straight over the back would be great,' Tim responded. 'We'll tilt the seat back and get a backboard in.'

'Right. We'll get the roof off as soon as we've dealt with these doors.'

Jason looked up at the tarpaulin a colleague was unfolding nearby. 'Things are going to get a bit noisy and messy now, sweetheart,' he told Courtney. 'We're going to cover you up so you don't get hit by any bits of glass or anything.'

Her eyes snapped open. 'Don't leave me.'

'I won't. I'll be right here with you under the covers.' Jason winked. 'My favourite spot when I'm with a gorgeous girl like you.'

'That'd be right.' The grin from his colleague acknowledged the kind of humour and encouragement that only Jason could get away with. Even Laura smiled. He'd be saying the same thing if the accident victim were a seventy-five-year-old grandmother of eight and it would probably have the same effect of keeping their patient comforted and calm.

'We'll need a dash roll as well,' Tim told the fire chief. 'We've got a leg trapped.'

'No problem. You staying in there, Laura?'

'May as well.' She moved back to a position where she could support Courtney's head and neck again. Only she knew that her comment referred to more than providing company for the victim. This was the only way Laura would ever get under any covers with Jason Halliday, but she wasn't complaining. Any job where she got to work with this particular fire crew was a bonus, and being one on one with a patient and only Jason was the closest they had ever worked together.

The car rocked and shook as hydraulic cutting gear was used to open it up like a giant sardine can. Tiny shards of glass peppered the tarpaulin sheltering those still inside the vehicle, and Laura made sure she kept Courtney's head immobile. A more violent rocking motion occurred as the roof was lifted clear of the car and Laura could hear the grin in Jason's voice.

'The earth sure moved for me. How're you doing, Courtney?'

'I'm fine.'

Amazingly, the injured girl *did* sound fine and Laura's lips curved a little, unseen in the darkness of their covering. Jason's somewhat unorthodox communication skills were a new experience and, surprisingly, she liked them. Six months ago she wouldn't have believed it could be remotely possible to add humour or—heaven forbid—*flirting* to an accident scene with beneficial results, but it worked. The

Green Watch fire crew of Inglewood station were a closely bonded team of intelligent and dedicated firemen and Jason, in particular, had a gift of lightening even the grimmest of atmospheres.

He had his work cut out for him in the next few minutes as the tarpaulin was removed and the rescue shifted into a higher gear. The car was now completely open to the elements with the windscreen, roof and doors removed. The pre-dawn chill was noticeable and scene time had already been nearly twenty minutes. Everyone wanted to move as quickly as possible now and get their patient to the medical care she needed.

The dash roll that lifted crushed metal from Courtney's right leg revealed a nasty compound fracture of her tib-fib. She tried to move her leg as the weight was lifted but her foot was trapped beneath the brake pedal and she screamed as her pain level skyrocketed. The blood loss was also increasing. Laura opened the flow on the IV fluids she now had running.

'Can you draw up another 10 milligrams of morphine, Tim?'

'Got it here,' her partner responded. 'Ready for the backboard?'

'Not yet. Her foot's still trapped.'

'I can deal with that.' Jason still had a heavy protective glove on one hand. He reached carefully past the gaping wound on Courtney's leg to ease his fingers between her foot and the top of the pedal. Only Laura noticed the way the lines deepened at the corners of his eyes. To anyone else he must have made bending the pedal upwards far enough to clear the trapped foot appear effortless.

'Ah-h-h! It *hurts*!'

'Almost there, love.' Jason's tone was calmly reassuring. 'We're going to tip your seat back now and slide a board underneath you.'

Too many figures were crowding in now and Courtney's grip on Jason's hand was lost as they finally lifted her clear of the wreck.

'BP was 80 systolic five minutes ago,' Laura told Tim. 'We need to get another line in.'

'Hare traction on that femur before we roll?'

Laura nodded. The low blood pressure could well be caused by the blood loss associated with the fractured bones Courtney had sustained. It was a two-person job to apply a traction splint so it wasn't something that could be done *en route*. It would mean a delay of another few minutes before transporting, but effective splinting would help control further blood loss and was therefore a priority.

It wasn't just the fire officers of Green Watch she was lucky to be working with, Laura decided as the ambulance rolled clear of the accident scene only three minutes later. Tim was one of the most competent paramedics she had ever had as a partner and they were perfectly matched to remain calm and efficient in virtually any circumstances. A few years over Laura's twenty-nine, Tim had the added advantage of more experience and he also had the kind of laid-back personality that made him fit in seamlessly at Inglewood station despite being in a different emergency service. He was just one of the boys.

As was Laura now. The novelty of having a female officer on the watch had worn off rapidly. A shade too rapidly maybe, but who could blame them for losing any interest her gender might have sparked? And it didn't matter. She was part of a great team and she'd be delighted to be considered an honorary bloke if only it wasn't for—

'How's it going back there?'

'Fine.' Laura scribbled down the update of recordings she'd been making automatically as her mind wandered. 'BP's up—100 over 60. Oxygen saturation is 98 per cent on 15 litres. Sinus tachy at 110.'

'We'll be at the hospital in about eight minutes.'

'OK. I'll radio through in a minute.' Laura turned back to her patient. 'How's the pain score out of ten now, Courtney?'

'About four, I guess.'

'That's a lot better but I'll give you a little bit more morphine. I'd like to get it down to at least two if I can.'

Caring for a multi-trauma patient *en route* gave little time to attend to paperwork so Laura completed the task using a spare patch of counter in the trauma room as the emergency department staff assessed the new arrival. By the time she was finished, X-rays had been completed and Courtney was being readied for Theatre where the orthopaedic surgeon would need to deal with the open lower leg fracture and the dislocation-fracture of her right elbow. Laura paused on her way out with the completed paperwork.

'All the best, Courtney. You're in good hands. You've got one of the best orthopaedic surgeons in town coming in to fix you up.'

'I just want to get it over with,' Courtney groaned. 'But thanks…for everything.'

'You're very welcome.'

'And can you thank that fireman for me? What was his name?'

'Jase. Jason Halliday.'

'Yeah, that's him. He was fantastic.'

'I'll tell him.' Laura had to suppress a wistful smile. It wasn't something she could tell Jason herself, no matter how much she might agree with the sentiment.

'How old is Jason?'

Perhaps Laura would also need to tell him that his techniques of distracting a patient had long-lasting effects. Courtney didn't look as though she was thinking about her injuries or impending surgery at all right now.

'Ancient.' Laura smiled. 'Pushing forty.'

'Oh…he didn't seem that old.'

Laura wasn't really lying. Anything over thirty was on the way to forty, wasn't it? And thirty-two was still far too old for a nineteen-year-old.

'He's really nice, isn't he?'

'Mmm. I'd better go now, Courtney. Looks like they're nearly ready to move you.'

Tim appeared in the trauma room doorway. 'We're all cleaned up and ready to go,' he told Laura. 'And I can almost smell Mrs M.'s bacon and eggs. You ready?'

Laura was more than ready to head back and finish her shift but her most recent patient wasn't quite ready to let her go.

'I couldn't really see what he looked like with that uniform and everything. Is he cute?'

'Cute' wasn't the word Laura would have chosen. Jason Halliday could be used as a pinup model for the fire service any day. Six feet two inches with a build to match his height. Sun-streaked, curly hair, dark blue eyes and a killer smile. There was only one word to describe Jason and that was…perfect.

'Imagine your typical surfer and add ten years and a pot belly.'

'Oh… He said he wasn't married, though, didn't he? Has he got a girlfriend?'

''Fraid so.' Laura's smile was not without sympathy but she escaped without offering any consolation in the face of Courtney's obvious disappointment. She could have said that Maxine was only a newbie and might not last long but what was the point? She knew only too well the strength of attraction Jason Halliday could inspire and this teenager had as much hope of sparking a reciprocal interest as she herself had.

Well, maybe that was wishful thinking. Courtney was slim, probably several inches taller than Laura's five feet two inches and her hair was an attractive russet rather than dead mouse, but even so she didn't measure up to Jason's usual standards in female companions. Better to be briefly disappointed now than to carry a torch and find the flame not only refused to get extinguished but simply burned a little brighter with every passing week.

'Jase is going to kill you when he hears about that ''pot belly'' remark,' Tim informed her a few minutes later.

'Only if you tell him,' Laura countered. She indicated a right turn and slowed the ambulance as she reached the main route back to their station. 'And if you do, *I'll* tell Mrs Mack who walked over her clean lino with those muddy boots last week.'

'You wouldn't!' Tim's expression feigned fear. Then he grinned. 'OK, my lips are sealed.' He tipped his head back and closed his eyes wearily. 'Can't say I blame you for trying to put her off. We get quite enough women turning up asking for our Jase as it is.' His tone became thoughtful. 'I wonder what it's like to be so compellingly attractive to the opposite sex?'

'Boring,' Laura said firmly. 'You can have too much of a good thing, you know.'

'No.' Tim sounded almost wistful now. 'I wouldn't know.'

Laura snorted softly. 'Join the club, Tim. I think I'm the founding member.'

'Oh, come on. I don't believe that for a minute.' Tim's quiet voice was suddenly serious. 'You're great, Laura. Best partner I've ever had. You're a brilliant paramedic, you've got a terrific sense of humour and…and your smile's lovely.'

'Thanks.' Laura's wry tone acknowledged the hesitation before Tim had found something physical to praise. 'I'm also short, fat and I wear glasses.'

'So?'

'So men don't make passes at girls who wear glasses.'

Tim's snort was much more definite than Laura's had been. He grinned again. 'So take them off when you want someone to make a pass at you.'

Laura laughed. If only it was that easy. Even the wry amusement lifted her spirits, however. 'Has anyone ever told you that you're a nice person, Tim?'

'Nah. The last woman that dumped me had a considerable command of adjectives that let me know precisely how boring I am.'

'You're not boring, Tim.' Laura pulled the ambulance to a halt and then started backing into the garage. 'You're dependable. Safe.'

'Ha! Safe is pretty close to boring if you ask me. Women want excitement, not safety.'

'There's a woman out there who's going to find safe pretty exciting.' Laura smiled at Tim. 'Hey, you're the best partner I've ever had. I love working with you.' It was just such a shame it hadn't been Tim she'd fallen in love with, but life was never that neat, was it?

'We do have fun, don't we?'

'Sure do. I can't believe I've been here for six months already. Seems like only last week I was wondering what it would be like to be stationed with a fire crew instead of just ambulance.' Laura climbed out of the driver's seat and walked around to join Tim at the back of the vehicle. 'I still haven't got over how funny *they* are, though.'

'What?'

'The boots.' Laura pointed to where the crew's heavy footwear was lined up, the tops of the boots protruding through the rolled-down legs of protective over-trousers. 'It looks for all the world like a crew was standing around the truck and they all got vaporised by some alien force or something.'

'Makes for a quick getaway.'

'I know.' Laura had seen Jason and his colleagues respond to a call. Feet slid into boots, over-trousers were yanked up and secured by elastic braces, and matching, heavy, mustard-yellow jackets with reflecting stripes were grabbed from the locker room along with helmets. The items of protective outer clothing were always left in precisely the same position on returning to the station, which left the officers wearing their uniforms of black trousers and navy blue T-shirts emblazoned with the red and white fire service logo.

As they were now. Laura and Tim had elected to wait until closer to the end of their shift before restocking and cleaning the ambulance. They had enough supplies if they got another call, and tempting fate by having a freshly prepared truck for the oncoming crew was not a good idea this close to their finishing time of seven a.m. A late call after a busy night such as they'd just had would not be welcome.

They entered the old house through the automatic side door that now joined it to the large, purpose-built garaging. The spacious lounge that ran nearly the whole width of the lower floor had become a common room, filled with comfortable furniture. The couches and chairs were being well patronised by weary men at the moment, half of whom had their feet resting on the coffee-tables. The other half had their footwear resting on the arms of the couches.

'In the name of St Bride!' Laura did her best to imitate the broad accent that fifty years of living in New Zealand hadn't dampened in Mrs McKendry's case. 'How many times do I have to tell you boys to keep your dratted feet off that furniture?'

To her delight, the accent and surprise factor were enough to initiate a guilty leap into compliance. Her laughter caused more than one head to turn, and then the amusement was general.

'Good one, Laura!' Tim shook his head at the firemen. 'You should have seen yourselves jump!'

'Lucky I didn't scream,' Cliff complained. 'She's just as scary as Mrs M.'

'Ah…but can she cook bacon and eggs?'

'And polish the furniture?'

'And get nasty stains out of any clothes?'

'Even Mrs M. couldn't get the stains out of your underwear, Stick.'

Laura shook her head and flopped into the nearest available armchair during the laughter that followed the last flippant remark. Maybe she was just too tired to feel amused. Or maybe the idea that she might measure up to the perfect housekeeper cut a little too close to the bone. She could do all those things but she wasn't going to be some man's housekeeper ever again. Not when that ended up being the main attraction she possessed.

Several pairs of eyes were fastened on the wall clock.

'It's 6.15.'

'Mmm. That bacon will be in the pan any minute now.'

'Why don't you do it for yourselves for once?'

That wasn't a suggestion one of the boys would have considered making. Laura found she had caused a brief but rather surprised silence. Jason looked positively bewildered.

'What...and make Mrs M. feel like she's not wanted?'

Laura's sigh revealed that she didn't have the energy to try and re-educate the men around her. Maybe it was an impossible task anyway. Was that why John had never lifted a finger in the kitchen? Or the bathroom, or anywhere else for that matter? Had he, in fact, been a kind and caring partner who had simply been trying to show her how much he'd needed her? *Ha!*

'She *would* be upset.' Tim's glance was speculative and Laura knew she deserved the gentle reprimand. The men of Inglewood station might complain and joke about Jean McKendry when she wasn't around, but she was part of the family if anyone else tried it. And the kitchen was strictly her domain during her 'office' hours.

'We've never *asked* her to do any of the stuff she does for us, you know,' Bruce added. 'She's just become an institution—ever since she popped over with a plate of scones the day this station opened five years ago.'

'Yeah, it just grew.' Cliff nodded. 'By the end of the year she was here every day, all day, cleaning and cooking.'

'And making sure we all had a clean hanky.'

'At least she gets paid for it now,' Bruce told Laura. 'And we all put in to buy all the food she insists on cooking us.'

'She loves us,' Jason said. He still looked puzzled. 'She *wants* to do it.'

'I know.' Laura smiled. 'She's wonderful and we're the envy of any other peripheral city station. Sorry.' She pushed her glasses up and rubbed the bridge of her nose. 'I'm just tired, I guess, and from where I'm sitting it's easy to take offence at the idea of a perfect woman's attributes being how easy she can make life for others.'

The second brief silence had a contrite air to it.

'Hey, we weren't getting at *you*, Laura.'

'No...we don't think of you as a woman.'

'Gee, thanks.' Not only was she the only member of Green Watch not to have earned some kind of nickname, they didn't even see her as being female.

'That wasn't helpful, Stick,' Jason said firmly. He gave Laura one of his killer smiles. 'What he meant was that you're one of us.'

'One of the boys,' Bruce put in kindly.

'No.' Jason sounded even firmer. 'Laura is most definitely not a boy. Heck, even I'm not *that* blind.'

Laura couldn't help smiling. Or help the pathetic little glow that started somewhere inside at the thought that Jason had not only noticed her femininity, he was defending her. Then her smile faded. What had the comment really meant…that it was really so hard to see anything attractive about her?

'We're not really chauvinistic,' Bruce said a little defensively. 'But this job requires people with pretty assertive personalities. So does yours. You wouldn't expect a firefighter who's risked life and limb to pull someone from a burning house or cut open a wrecked vehicle to extricate the injured to go home and bake a cake or clean a toilet, would you?'

'Why not? You'd expect me to,' Laura told them. 'I've just been squished inside a car wreck looking after the injured, but I bet you wouldn't put up too much of a fight if I offered to go and make you all coffee or throw some bacon and eggs together.'

'Mmm.' The sound was a frustrated groan. 'Bacon and eggs!'

'Don't worry, Laura,' Tim said. 'We all know you're just as much of a hero as we are.'

'Yeah.' Cliff winked at her. 'Maybe you need a wife as well.'

Laura gritted her teeth. She knew they were teasing her but it was easy to think that her protest had not made the slightest impression on any prejudice held by these men. And what did it matter, anyway? She couldn't imagine being attracted to a man who was keen to bake cakes or clean toilets. She'd never wanted to find a sensitive New Age guy. She was just twisted and bitter because John had never really wanted her for herself. Apart from the freely available sex, he would probably have been happier being married to Jean McKendry.

Jason seemed to have picked up at least part of her thoughts by telepathy.

'You should also know,' he said seriously, 'that we don't consider Mrs M. to be the *perfect* woman.'

'No.' Stick grinned. 'She's about forty years past her use-by date.'

'And she's grumpy as hell.'

'Yeah.' Jason rubbed his elbow reflectively. 'She hit me with a wooden spoon the other day.'

'Well, you *were* sticking your dirty, fat finger in her gravy.'

'I was only tasting it.'

The mention of food provoked another general glance towards the clock and yet another short silence.

'What was that?' Laura frowned at the faint but noticeably unusual sound.

'Just a cat.'

'Gate squeaking?' Cliff suggested hopefully. 'Mrs M. arriving for breakfast?'

'Jeez, we'd better not get another callout,' Jason said unhappily. 'I'm *starving*.'

'You're always starving, Jase.'

'Can't help it. I'm a growing lad.'

'We've noticed.' Stick leaned over the side of the chair and poked Jason's midriff. 'You'd better watch out, mate. Pot belly city!'

Laura's lips twitched as she gave Tim a warning glance. He grinned and raised his eyebrows as though acknowledging that Laura might have already been provocative enough, especially for this time of day.

They were all startled at the sound made by the original back door of the house. Not that it wasn't Mrs McKendry's normal entrance-way, but she didn't usually open and shut it with quite such purpose. The room fell uncomfortably silent now. Mrs M. wasn't happy. Someone had upset her and they were all likely to suffer the consequences. Laura was suddenly acutely aware of just how right her colleagues had been not to trespass on their housekeeper's self-designated areas of responsibility.

Never mind the culinary and other benefits they all received—letting Jean McKendry think she was indispensable was actually an act of kindness. Looking after Inglewood station was her life and while she could be nosy, grumpy and always opinionated, she was never unfair. If she was this upset there would be a good reason for it.

The determined tap of sensible, low-heeled shoes got louder as Mrs McKendry traversed the kitchen's linoleum floor. All eyes were drawn to the arched opening that joined the dining-room end of the lounge to the kitchen that ran along the other side of the house. Those same eyes swivelled in unison to the large cardboard box that Mrs M. deposited carefully on the table. Wiry arms were now folded in front of the small woman's spare frame. And, in case her body language wasn't enough to let them know that this time they were in serious trouble, her tone backed it up more than adequately.

'I'm waiting,' she snapped.

'What for, Mackie?' Jason's smile was one of his most winning. It wasn't even directed at Laura and it was enough to melt *her* bones. Using the affectionate nickname had to be overkill, surely? 'What have we done?'

'I know *what* one of you has done,' Mrs M. enunciated with precision. 'What I want to know is, *who* is responsible?'

'Who is responsible for *what*?'

A sound rather similar to a cat's mew or a gate squeaking was suddenly produced by the box on the table. Mrs McKendry's lips almost disappeared into a straight, grim line.

'*Who* is responsible for this puir wee bairn being left on the back doorstep of Inglewood station?'

CHAPTER TWO

A SPELL had been cast.

Laura experienced an odd sensation, as though a wand had actually been waved over the group of people sitting in the lounge of the Inglewood emergency response station. An electric tingle—a feeling she was unable to identify on the spectrum between elation and fear—ran through her entire body, and she knew without a shadow of doubt that the axis of her world was tilting.

Only an insignificant amount of time followed Mrs McKendry's startling demand but it marked the transition between normal life and something totally unknown. One minute they had all been slumped in various positions of rest, filling in time and carefully not tempting fate by saying they were probably safe from the disruption of a late callout, and now they were suddenly involved in a disruption that was completely without precedent.

Laura wasn't the only one to be stunned. Or to feel nervous in taking that first step of an unknown journey. The whole of Green Watch was moving. Slowly, silently, they approached the box on the table with as much caution as if it contained a live cobra.

Stick was the first to open his mouth. His nickname had been derived from affectionate ribbing that he'd been hit more than once by the ugly one. Right now, his pock-marked face had softened dramatically and his incredulous smile was almost as large as his nose.

'It's a *baby*!'

The murmur was probably intended to be a personal observation but the silence surrounding him was so profound the words might as well have been shouted.

'Go to the top of the class, Stick.' Bruce grinned.

'Is it a girl or a boy?' Tim queried.

'It's not colour-coded,' Jason complained. 'How are we supposed to know?'

'Change its nappy,' Cliff advised knowledgeably.

'Not on your life!' Jason held both hands up, palms outwards, and leaned back to emphasise the invisible barrier. 'I don't *do* babies.'

'Someone did,' Mrs McKendry snapped. Her arms were still folded and she was tapping one foot impatiently. 'And I'd like to know *who*.'

'Wasn't me,' Jason declared firmly.

'Or me,' Stick and Cliff said simultaneously.

'Definitely wasn't me.' Tim raised an eyebrow at Laura and she smiled. Having a baby dumped on your doorstep certainly wasn't a boring thing to happen.

'I should be so lucky,' Bruce sighed.

They all stared at the infant. Fluffy, dark blue polar fleece fabric with cute yellow ducks on it had been folded to form a mattress in the box. The baby had been wrapped in a blanket of the same fleece but tiny limbs had been active enough to loosen the covering and miniature hands could be seen poking from the armholes of a white stretch suit. A tiny fist threatened to clout its owner's cheek but somehow it escaped causing pain and settled against a questing mouth instead. Surprisingly loud sucking noises filled the new silence and large dark blue eyes stared up fearlessly at the crowd of faces leaning over the box.

'It's hungry.' As a father of three, Cliff was entitled to take the lead as far as experience in such matters went.

'Could be hereditary.' Stick gave one of his usual cheerful grins. 'Who's always hungry around here?'

'Don't look at me!' Jason's eyes widened in alarm. 'I told you, I don't do babies. I'm careful, man. Always have been.'

'There's always one that slips through the net.'

There was a ripple of laughter. 'Especially when the catch is that big!'

'It *has* got blond hair,' Bruce observed. 'Except I don't suppose it means that much at this age.'

'How old do you reckon it is?'

For some reason everyone looked at Laura. Was she supposed to know the answer due to some feminine intuition? Had she always been lumped in the 'motherly type' basket? Or had everybody simply noticed how quiet she'd been so far? Cliff wasn't about to be outdone in the knowledge stakes, however.

'It's pretty newly hatched, I'd say. Two or three weeks?'

Laura caught her breath but her reaction had nothing to do with the thought of such a young baby being abandoned. She had just realised why the baby's face was so fascinating.

The eyes weren't really that dark. They were blue, certainly. A lovely sort of cornflower blue. They gave the initial appearance of darkness because of the edging to the iris, which was a shade deep enough to compete with the pupil. Why had nobody else noticed such an obvious genetic link to a potential parent in this group of men? There was only one person who had eyes like that.

And they were *exactly* like that.

Another frisson of an unidentifiable emotion caught Laura unexpectedly. Jealousy, perhaps? No. It was more like a feeling of connection to that baby. A longing to touch it. To pick it up. When the little fist was suddenly flung free of the sucking mouth and a tiny face crumpled and reddened she had no hesitation in reaching into the box.

Nobody else was going to do it, she told herself. The men were backing off in alarm at the deterioration in the baby's mood. At her touch, the screwed-up face relaxed and the tiny fist unfurled to encompass her finger. Laura smiled into a carbon copy of Jason Halliday's eyes.

'Hello, there,' she whispered.

Only a few short minutes had passed since Mrs McKendry had dropped this bombshell in their midst but it was very unusual that the older woman had not yet said more than she had. Nobody was surprised to hear her begin to issue some firm instructions.

'Sit down at this table—every last one of you. I don't care if half of Wellington burns to the ground. You're no' going anywhere till we get to the bottom of this.'

Amazingly, the whole group of burly, dedicated firefighters complied. They were all out of their depth right now and it clearly came as a relief for their self-appointed surrogate mother to take charge.

'We should call the police,' Bruce suggested mildly. 'It's a criminal offence to leave a baby unattended.'

The look he received questioned his level of intelligence rather eloquently. 'Whoever left this bairn had reason to think it *would* be attended to.'

A dainty foot tapped on linoleum in the silence that followed.

'And there can be only one explanation for that. One of you is this baby's father.'

'*You're* lucky.' Jason's comment was directed at Laura, who, along with Mrs McKendry, was the only person now standing. 'It can't be yours. I think we would have noticed.'

The chuckle of appreciation at the attempt to lift the atmosphere was short-lived and it hadn't even raised a smile as far as Laura was concerned. Carrying a full-term baby may well have made her large enough for Jason to notice. In fact, it was probably the only way he'd really notice her as a woman.

As though her resentment was contagious, the baby emitted a fractious cry and Laura did what she'd been wanting to do ever since she'd first seen what was in the box. She scooped the baby up and cradled it in her arms.

It was crying in earnest now and there was no doubt it was well overdue for a nappy change but Laura didn't mind. The slight weight of the infant in her arms triggered an instinctive and remarkably fierce desire to protect and comfort it. She rocked her noisy, smelly bundle and directed soothing words towards its ear. The words she spoke were unimportant. So was what was being said around her for the next few moments.

The first Red Watch arrivals to take over the day shift started to form a secondary tier of astonished spectators. As far as these men were concerned they were not involved. The baby had been left during the night, therefore it had to be someone on Green Watch who was implicated as the father. Some even found the situation highly amusing.

'No wonder someone left it on the doorstep. Noisy little bugger, isn't it?'

'Don't get too close. It doesn't smell great either.'

'Let's put it back where Mrs Mack found it.' The speaker suddenly thought of an urgent job that needed attending to as he felt the heat of Jean McKendry's glare.

'I still think we should call the police,' Bruce said heavily. 'Or Social Welfare. We can't sit here all day, Mrs M. We've had a busy night shift and what we need is some sleep.'

'What *she* needs is feeding,' Laura informed them. How she knew it was a girl was not questioned.

'Bacon and eggs?' Jason suggested hopefully. They all looked at Mrs McKendry but any prospect of a cooked breakfast evaporated instantly on reading her face.

'I'll make some toast,' someone on Red Watch offered. 'Have you guys cleaned the truck?'

'We're not allowed to move,' Stick responded gloomily. 'Not until one of us owns up to fathering this kid.'

'Don't worry.' Red Watch members were backing away now. 'We'll do it.'

The new crew for the ambulance day shift was equally co-operative. Helpful, even.

'We could go out and find some formula or something at the supermarket.'

The pager messages signalling a priority-one callout to a chest pain put an end to that scheme. Within another few minutes the hooter sounded to alert the fire crew.

'Alarm sounding at a warehouse on the corner of George and Matton streets,' the loudspeaker announced. 'Smoke seen to be coming from the rear of the building.'

Green Watch members could see the departing vehicles through the dining-room's window. They listened to the fading sirens with almost defeated expressions.

'This isn't getting us anywhere,' Bruce declared finally. 'Look, Mrs M. If one of us had any idea that we were related to this baby we would have said so by now.'

Raised eyebrows and pursed lips suggested that this was not necessarily an accurate assumption.

'Half of us are married. We've got families of our own.'

'Precisely. A good reason not to confess, wouldn't you say?'

Laura was jiggling an increasingly unhappy infant now. No one knew how long this baby had been outside in the box. It might have been hours since its last feed. Her reluctance to cast the first stone was wearing thinner by the minute. If this carried on any longer she was going to open her mouth and point out the obvious. Why hadn't anyone else noticed yet? She shifted the baby's weight slightly and became aware that the patch of blanket under her arm was distinctly damp.

'Stick, could you get that other blanket out of the box?' Laura asked. 'She's leaking a bit and getting cold won't make her any happier.'

'Hope you've got gloves on.' Jason blinked at the look he received from Laura. 'Hey! What have *I* done?'

He found out soon enough. As Stick pulled the folded fleece from the box his eyes widened.

'There's stuff in here,' he exclaimed. 'A bottle and a tin of baby food. There's nappies and— What the hell is this?'

The piece of paper said it all. Officially stamped by the authority vested in the registrar of births, deaths and marriages, it gave all the information Mrs McKendry had been waiting for. She peered at the certificate and then transferred a steely gaze to one of the men staring anxiously back.

'Jason Halliday. What have you got to say for yourself *now*?'

'Huh?'

The piece of paper was passed along the table and everyone had scanned it by the time Bruce handed it to Jason.

'Here you go...*Dad*.'

Jason's colour had faded to give his bewilderment a decidedly pale background. He stared at the birth certificate, with his name handwritten on the empty line for 'Father's

Name', for a seemingly interminable length of time. It became too long for his audience.

'Megan's a nice name,' Cliff said hesitantly.

'It's her one-month birthday today,' Bruce added.

'She was born in England,' Stick said kindly. 'You can't really be blamed for having missed the big event, Jase.'

Laura said nothing. She reached into the box and extracted a disposable nappy, some wipes and a clean stretchsuit. She could still see Jason when she moved towards one of the couches to find room to put the baby down. She could see growing consternation replacing shocked disbelief.

'So.' Mrs McKendry looked up from where she was reading the instructions on the tin of formula. 'I take it you were no' informed about this baby's existence, Jason?'

'No. Someone's made a mistake.' Jason rested his forehead on the palms of both hands. 'A really *big* mistake.'

Bruce reached for the certificate again. 'The mother's name is Shelley. Shelley Bates.'

'I don't know any Shelleys,' Jason said miserably. 'Never have.'

'It says here that her occupation is a model.'

Laura wasn't the only one to see how well that fitted.

'You've been out with plenty of models, Jase.'

'I don't sleep with them all,' Jason said defensively. 'In fact, I haven't had a good s—' He stopped abruptly, glanced up at Mrs McKendry who was still standing at the other end of the table, groaned and buried his face in his hands again. 'It doesn't matter,' he muttered.

Laura disagreed. She was very interested to hear that Jason didn't have sex with every female that gave him the opportunity. She stuck down the tabs to hold the fresh nappy secure. She would also very much like to know how long it had been since he'd had a good... whatever crude noun he'd been tempted to use to describe the experience. It couldn't have been more than ten months ago, that was for sure.

'I guess *we're* off the hook.' Bruce yawned. 'We could go home now, eh, Mrs Mack?'

'No!' Jason's face appeared again. 'I don't know anyone called Shelley and I haven't been in England for six years. This *has* to be a mistake.'

'Why would someone make a mistake like that?'

'Maybe it didn't happen in England,' Cliff said thoughtfully. 'Maybe Shelley whoever she is was in New Zealand on holiday.'

'A holiday with Halliday.' Stick chuckled. His smile faded rapidly as he realised his quip was not appreciated.

'I don't care where Shelley was. Or who she was with. It wasn't *me*.'

'The bairn's four weeks old.' Mrs McKendry had moved to the kitchen bench and was spooning formula into the bottle. 'That means she was conceived about nine to ten months ago.'

'December,' Stick said helpfully. 'No... more like late January.'

'Let's say New Year, give or take a week or two.'

'Can you remember that far back, Jase?'

'You were going out with Britney,' Cliff declared. 'I remember *her*. Red hair and legs up to her—'

'That was March. We broke up at Easter when we had an argument about chocolate bunnies.'

'OK, what about Melissa? You know, the one with those Pamela Anderson—'

'She was after Britney,' Jason interrupted swiftly. 'I think.'

'No…I'm sure she was the one that came to that barbecue we had on the beach in February. Yellow bikini?'

Laura hadn't forgotten that yellow bikini— or the assets it had supported. She glanced up from fastening the snaps on the stretchsuit, intending to direct a 'you know you deserve everything that's coming' glance, but to her astonishment, the tips of Jason's ears were bright pink. Good grief—the man was embarrassed!

He *should* be ashamed of himself if he couldn't even remember the order or names of the string of women in his life. Maybe this was the first occasion he'd ever had to consider the repercussions of such an active social life. Or maybe he was disturbed by the wider picture he was currently having to confront. In any case, Laura liked the fact that he was embarrassed. She picked up the baby again and her lips curved into a smile against the soft wisps of blonde hair.

'Daddy's blushing,' she whispered. 'How about that?'

'Daddy' was still fielding a list of potential conquests that might have had confusing names.

'What about Charlotte?'

'*Sounds* a bit like Shelley.'

Despite the spotlight being so firmly on Jason, even Bruce, who was stifling frequent yawns, was not about to leave his fellow fire-fighter in the lurch and go home for some well-deserved rest. Stick shook his head sorrowfully.

'This should be a lesson to us all. Anyone could just scribble in our names on some bloody birth certificate.'

'Speak for yourself, mate. I'm happily married.'

'DNA,' Cliff said with relief. 'You could get a test, Jase, and prove it's not yours.'

'That could take weeks! What the hell am I supposed to do with it in the meantime?'

'Maybe the mother's only gone shopping or something. She could be back any minute.'

'Yeah, right. Like she's come all the way from England for a spot of shopping and she leaves the baby on a doorstep in the middle of the night so she doesn't have to bother finding a babysitter.'

Laura sat down at the table and Mrs McKendry silently handed her the bottle of formula. Tentatively, she poked the teat into the baby's mouth and to her delight it was accepted enthusiastically.

'Well, that's a blessing,' Mrs McKendry said. 'At least she's used to a bottle.'

Laura could feel the rhythmic tug of the sucking movements. The baby's wide-eyed gaze fastened onto hers as though she was receiving the nourishment via some kind of visual connection. Laura found herself smiling.

'Oh…she's gorgeous!'

'Aye.' Jean McKendry's expression softened noticeably. Then she pushed her spectacles more firmly onto the bridge of her nose and leaned a little closer to peer at the baby's face.

'It was *Sharon*!' Jason announced.

'What was?'

'The woman who's set me up. It has to be.' Jason nodded to confirm his own statement. 'A girl from England that I met when I had that summer holiday in the Coromandel.'

'Sure it wasn't Shelley?'

Jason frowned in concentration. 'She had a sister and I remember that their names were alike enough to be confusing. It was a bit of a joke and they didn't mind when I got it wrong.' Jason nodded again, more slowly this time. 'That must be where this has come from. Sharon's sister has had a baby and they've decided to name me as the father.'

'Maybe they want to emigrate or something,' Cliff suggested.

'Of course, that's what it'll be. It's pretty hard to get into the country and having a New Zealand father for a child is probably a great start.'

'Marrying the New Zealand father would have been a much safer plan,' Laura said dryly. 'I mean, writing in your name like that doesn't make you the legal father. Why didn't she turn up months ago?'

'Dunno.' Jason shrugged. 'Maybe the sisters didn't get together and come up with the plan until after the baby was born.'

'How much alike did these sisters look, Jase?'

'Identical. They were twins. Long blonde hair and cute accents. Young, though. I think they were only about nineteen.' Jason rubbed the back of his neck as though something was hurting. 'I suppose it *could* have been Shelley. Names didn't actually seem that important at the time.'

The sniff that emanated from Mrs McKendry's direction was an expression of frank disapproval.

'It was only one night,' Jason sighed. 'There was this big beach party. Hey, I was on holiday. You're supposed to have a good time on holiday!'

'Not *that* good,' Stick said enviously.

'And not with twins!' Tim sounded appalled.

'It wasn't with *both* of them. It was... I was... Oh, *hell*.' Jason closed his eyes with apparent exhaustion. 'It doesn't matter. I can't be the father.' He stood up. 'You were right, Bruce. Let's hand this problem to the police. For all we know this baby's been abducted and the birth certificate is some sort of nasty practical joke.'

'It's no joke.' Mrs McKendry had simply been waiting for a gap in the rapid-fire conversation between the men. 'And you might as well stop your havering, Jason Halliday. This bairn is yours.'

'How can you say that?' Jason's astonishment at being betrayed by someone he trusted was directed at Mrs McKendry only briefly. Then it was transferred to Laura. '*You* think it's mine, too, don't you?'

Laura nodded. 'It's as plain as the nose on your face, I'm afraid, Jase. Or should I say the eyes.'

'What about them?' Jason asked faintly.

'Come and have a look.'

They all came and had a look. They stared at baby Megan and then at Jason. And one by one they all nodded slowly.

'It doesn't matter if it was Sharon or Shelley or bloody Madonna,' Stick said sadly. 'Yep. This kid's yours, all right, Jase.'

Laura couldn't help it. 'The eyes have it,' she murmured.

Jason wasn't amused. 'Lots of people have eyes with rings around them.'

'No.' Laura was careful to keep her tone perfectly neutral. 'Your eyes are actually quite unusual, Jase. And Megan's are a carbon copy.'

Jason sank into the chair opposite Laura. 'What am I going to *do*?'

You had to feel sorry for him, Laura decided. For someone like Jason who played almost as hard as he worked and made no secret of intending to enjoy his bachelor status for as long as possible, this had to be his worst nightmare. He looked defeated right now. Lost. And Laura couldn't help offering a sympathetic smile. Jason's forlorn gaze locked onto hers as though encouraging her to say something that might make this whole mess go away.

But it was Mrs McKendry who spoke and she wasn't going to let Jason off any hook. 'You're going to take responsibility for your child, that's what you're going to do,' she said crisply. 'Laura, hand the baby over to its father.'

'*No!* I'll drop it.'

'Don't be such a gowk,' Mrs McKendry snapped. 'Laura?'

She felt like an executioner but Mrs Mack was right. This was Jason's baby. His problem. He was now in such a shocked state he simply accepted the bundle Laura placed carefully into his arms. Then he stared at the baby's face with an even more forlorn expression.

For several seconds, father and daughter exchanged stares of equal intensity. Then Megan

Bates Halliday opened her tiny rosebud mouth and bellowed her disapproval.

'She doesn't like you much, does she?' Bruce observed unnecessarily.

'The feeling's probably mutual right now,' Stick said sympathetically.

'You lot...' Mrs McKendry peered over the top of her half-moon spectacles '...can all go home. You're no' helping and you need some sleep.'

'You're not wrong there.' Bruce rubbed his face and didn't bother hiding a yawn. 'I'm absolutely knackered.'

'Me, too,' Cliff sighed. 'Sorry, mate, but I'm going to have to head home and hit the sack.'

Megan's cries became louder and Tim stood up as well. 'You coming, Laura?'

'In a minute.' Laura couldn't abandon Jason. Not when he looked at her with that kind of mute appeal. He needed help.

Stick was clearly torn. He shared a house with Jason and another fireman, Mitch, from Red Watch. After an apologetic glance at Jason he turned to Mrs McKendry.

'I s'pose Jase is going to have to take this baby home with him if he has to look after it, isn't he?'

'I can't look after it. I don't know the first damn thing about babies.' Jason had to raise his voice over the increasing noise level. 'And we're not allowed pets, remember?'

'Your daughter's just been fed,' Mrs McKendry informed Jason. 'I expect she needs burping now.' Clicking her tongue at Jason's expression, she reached out. 'Like this!' She put the baby upright and rubbed her back. Megan obligingly belched loudly and sent a dribble of milk across the lacy collar of Mrs McKendry's blouse.

Stick stared in horrified fascination but Jason looked impressed. 'Hey, you know about babies, Mackie.'

'Well, I may no' have been blessed with any of my own but I've picked up the odd one or two in my time.'

'You could look after her.'

'No, Jason. This is *your* bairn.'

'I'll pay you.' Jason sounded desperate. He obviously didn't want to hold the baby again but he had no choice. It was simply pressed into his arms. 'I'll pay you anything you like!'

Mrs McKendry shook her head.

'But anyone can see she hates me.'

Stick took a step backwards as Megan started crying again. 'Look, mate. No offence but it's going to be hard to sleep with that noise in the house. I might stay on station.'

'I've got beds in my sleep-out if you want one of those,' Cliff offered.

'Sounds like a plan.' Stick gave Jason an apologetic grin. 'Sorry, mate...but...well, you know.'

'Yeah...' Jason sounded despondent. Then he looked beseechingly at Laura. 'I guess you're going to desert me, too. You probably think I deserve this.'

Laura held his gaze. 'What *I* think, Jason Halliday, is that you're in need of a friend right now.'

He still hadn't looked away. His daughter stopped howling as though her father's tentative smile had been enough to distract her. '*You'll* help me, Laura?'

He could see her. For the first time he could *really* see her. As a person rather than a profession. A valuable person. OK, so maybe that valuable person was a babysitter but beggars couldn't be choosers, could they?

'Yeah.' Laura smiled back. 'I'll help you, Jase.'

Jason was on his feet and somehow the baby was in her arms again, but Laura hardly registered the fact as Jason planted a kiss on her forehead.

'Laura Green, I love you.' His smile widened. 'Be back in a tick. I'm desperate to go to the loo.'

Jean McKendry gave Laura a steady glance. 'Och, hen, do you know what you're doing here?'

'I think I do.'

Laura was making herself indispensable, that was what she was doing. Jason was going to be very grateful but it wasn't his appreciation Laura sought. This was the first opportunity she'd ever had to spend time alone with him. Well…almost alone. If they had even a few hours together Jason might realise there was more to her than appearances suggested. And if that was too much to hope for, she would at least be able to give herself a lesson in distinguishing fantasy from reality and then move on with her life. It wasn't just the first opportunity. It was quite likely to be her *only* opportunity, and Laura had no intention of letting it slip through her fingers.

'Yes,' she said quietly. 'I'm sure I know what I'm doing.'

Disconcertingly, Laura had the impression that Mrs McKendry knew precisely what she had been thinking but if that was the case, she was being granted permission to carry on.

'If you run into real problems, call me,' the older woman said. 'And if the mother hasn't come back by the time you're both on duty again, I'll help during work hours.'

Green Watch had just completed two days and two nights on duty. It would be four days before the next day shift. Was there really a chance that Laura could have *that* much time alone with Jason and his daughter?

'Heavens, I'm sure the mother will be back long before then. Nobody could just leave their baby with a virtual stranger for that long.' Laura blinked at Mrs McKendry. 'Could they?' Her jaw dropped a fraction. 'You know something about this that you're not saying, don't you, Mrs Mack?'

'Let's just say that the bairn was no' on the doorstep for as long as I made out.'

'You *saw* her?' Laura breathed. 'You saw the mother leaving the box?'

'Not precisely.' Mrs McKendry lowered her voice. 'I saw a *man* leaving the box. Then he got back in the car and kissed a woman with long, blonde hair. Rather more thoroughly than the occasion called for, in my opinion. They drove off, laughing.' Her eyes narrowed in disgust. '*She* didn't look back. No' even *once*.'

'Did you get the number of the car?'

'No.'

Laura found it unlikely that such a detail would have escaped those sharp grey eyes but the implications were not escaping either of them. If the mother had callously abandoned her almost newborn baby and gone off with her lover, laughing, then it was highly unlikely they would be back in a hurry.

If at all.

A mix of emotion washed over Laura. Excitement. Hope. And a good dose of nervousness. This *was* her chance and she'd better be very careful not to screw it up.

'Why didn't you say something before?'

'I think Jason will have more than enough to cope with, thinking he's looking after his bairn on a very temporary basis. What do you think he would do if he thought there was any chance it was intended to be a more permanent arrangement?'

He'd run screaming into the middle distance, that was what. He'd call the police or Social Welfare and do whatever it took to side-step the responsibility. Informing the authorities was actually quite likely to be exactly what they should be doing at this point and Mrs Mack knew that as well as Laura did. So why was she doing this? To teach Jason Halliday a life lesson, perhaps? Or could she also see it as the opportunity Laura might otherwise never have had?

Jean McKendry smiled at her and Laura had her answer. She dropped her gaze to the baby in her arms, suddenly embarrassed that anyone could have guessed what she thought had been an increasingly well-guarded secret.

'Just remember, hen,' the housekeeper said softly. 'You're helping, no' taking over. You're no' this baby's mother, you know.' The pause seemed deliberate. 'You're no' Jason Halliday's mother either.'

'I'll remember,' Laura promised.

'If you turn yourself into a doormat you have only yourself to blame when people start wiping their feet all over you.'

Laura's swift glance was startled. Mrs McKendry was a fine one to talk about not mothering people. It was precisely the relationship this widow had with a great many men. Laura swallowed. Maybe that was why she did know what she was talking about. Had Mrs McKendry's marriage been as empty and unfulfilling as the relationship she herself would have had if she'd stayed with John?

The twinkle in Mrs McKendry's eyes seemed to be wishing her luck. 'Jason's got very big feet, hasn't he?'

Laura grinned. 'I'll make sure there's a very big doormat...outside the house.'

'You do that, hen.'

'What's Laura going to do?' Jason must have been splashing water on his face. Damp tendrils of blond-streaked curls clung to his forehead. Had he been hoping to wake himself up from a bad dream, perhaps?

'She's going to make a list of what you need to buy on the way home,' Mrs McKendry said brightly.

'A large bottle of gin?' But Jason's attempt at humour was half-hearted.

'Nappies,' he was informed sternly. 'And formula and some more clothes. And something for that bairn to sleep in.'

'Can't we just take the box home?'

Jason seemed to have aged ten years in the last hour but Laura could see through the faint edge of despair he was trying to cover with humour. He wasn't about to run away, no matter how unwelcome this situation was. In the face of total unwillingness and ignorance he was prepared to do what he had to do, and Laura loved him even more for the courage he was unwittingly displaying.

'Don't worry.' Laura stood up, holding a now sleeping infant. 'There's a baby's car seat in the ambulance storeroom. We'll borrow that for the day and Megan can sleep in it. There's enough formula and nappies to last until tomorrow and who knows?' Laura avoided looking at anyone but Jason. 'Maybe Shelley will be back by then.'

A ray of hope shone from Jason's smile. 'Shall...shall I hold it, then, while you go and find the seat thing?'

Laura bit back a wry smile as she handed Jason his daughter. 'She's not an "it", Jase. Her name is Megan.'

The bob of Jason's Adam's apple gave away his nervous swallow but, to his credit, he looked quite calm as he regarded the tiny peaceful face shrouded in blue polar fleece. He cleared his throat and spoke very softly.

'Hi, Megan...I'm Jase.' He cleared his throat again. 'Your...um...dad, I guess.'

Laura hurried towards the storeroom, swallowing rather hard herself to clear the unexpected prickle of tears. She had been right to think that something fundamental in her life had changed the moment Mrs McKendry had demanded an explanation for the unprecedented delivery to the station. The axis of her world had tilted so sharply she was in freefall right now.

It was scary because there was absolutely no way of knowing what condition she might be in when she found her feet again. But it was also exhilarating because what really mattered was that she wasn't alone. Baby Megan and her father were both coming along for the ride, and Laura intended to make the most of every possible moment.

CHAPTER THREE

'OH, WHAT a sweetie. How old is she?'

'Four weeks.'

'Look at those eyes!' The sales assistant at Baby Warehouse glanced up and Laura could swear the eyelashes fluttered. 'Just like Daddy's.'

'Yeah.' Any flutter had been lost on Jason. With more than twenty-four hours' practice, that trapped expression and tone was becoming almost normal.

'So, how's it going?' The sales assistant smiled brightly at Jason and then glanced at Laura. Her tone oozed sympathy. 'Incredibly tiring business, being new parents, isn't it?'

Laura looked down at the small face peeping out from the blue polar fleece blanket. Of course, *she* looked enough of a wreck to induce sympathy. The short, snatched periods of sleep between the dauntingly unfamiliar and full-on occupation of caring for such a young baby would take it out of anybody. Add the stress of being with somebody who was struggling to contain the desire to bail out, a house that was a prime example of how horrible three males could make their living environment and absolutely no baby equipment to make the job any easier, and she was nearly ready to bail out herself.

It had been precisely that threat that had finally persuaded Jason to come to this large specialist retail establishment.

'Either we get some gear or you're on your own, Jason Halliday,' she had said wearily that morning. Astonishingly, she had experienced only a muted tingle at the sight of Jason wearing nothing but a pair of ancient pyjama pants held loosely on his hips by a frayed cord. His bare, well-tanned chest had only a smattering of hair, the tips of which had been sunbleached to a pale gold. The shaft of desire had put up only a weak struggle against burgeoning resentment.

'I am *not* going to bathe this baby in a kitchen sink with a dishcloth that looks like it needs a government health warning slapped on it,' Laura had continued. 'And where the hell did these dishes come from? We spent two hours last night getting this bench cleared.' She'd known she'd sounded like a harpy or a nagging wife but she hadn't cared. The enthusiasm to make herself totally indispensable and show Jason just what a wonderful personality she had was wearing off with alarming rapidity.

'Just look at that!' The plate in question held the remnants of a meal that must have been abandoned a very long time ago. 'It's got so much fur growing on it, it looks like road kill.'

Jason's grin was very lopsided. 'I found it under my bed,' he admitted. 'And I found the rest when I was clearing out Stick's room so you had somewhere to sleep.' He rubbed the back of his hand against an unshaven chin. 'It's OK. I'll clean it all up.'

'You sure will,' Laura agreed. It was really quite easy to dismiss the faint rasping sound the chin rub had produced. The curiosity about what it would feel like to touch it herself was also fleeting enough to ignore. 'And when you've finished, we're going to find a baby shop. We need more formula, nappies, a bed, a bath and some toys.'

'Toys? Whatever for? All it does is eat and sleep and yell. You don't need toys for any of that. She's probably got buckets of toys at home.' Jason peered anxiously at Laura. 'You can't leave me. I wouldn't last five minutes without you.'

'You might if you actually learned how to change a nappy and hold a bottle instead of insisting that I do it.'

'But you're so good at it. You're a born mother, Laura. Megan loves you already.'

'Rubbish.' But Laura couldn't help the tiny glow of satisfaction seeping through the cracks of her exhaustion. She might have considered the term 'a born mother' a slur on her attractiveness before this, but even twenty-four hours had been enough to demonstrate the kind of qualities a mother needed. Confidence, compassion, patience, selflessness and a bucket of stamina. From now on she would consider the phrase a huge compliment.

'Besides,' Jason said persuasively, 'it's not going to be for much longer. If Shelley hasn't turned up in another day or so, we'll do something about it. Track her down and find out what's going on.'

The reminder was enough. Another glance at Jason allowed desire a stronger foothold and this time it was mixed with something new. Sympathy. Not that she could afford to feel too sorry for Jason. An echo of Mrs McKendry's warning sounded. Laura wasn't going to be a doormat for anyone ever again. Not even Jason Halliday. If this opportunity was going to provide what she hoped, however, she needed it to last as long as possible, and in order for any of them to survive they needed the help that the proper gear could provide.

'I don't care if it is only for another day, Jase.' Laura managed to sound pleasingly resolute. 'We have to get supplies. You can always give them to Megan when she goes.'

Jason sighed. 'Yeah. I guess I'm going to be in for paying some kind of child support. I suppose I could look on this like a down payment.'

'That's the spirit,' Laura said dryly. 'Don't forget to keep the receipts.'

Jason's face brightened. 'There you go. I wouldn't have thought of that. Thank goodness I've got you around to look out for me.'

'Just do the dishes, Jase. I'll see if Megan's other suit is dry enough to wear yet.'

So, here they were. Standing in a shop that boasted aisles and aisles of brightly coloured baby supplies in an astonishing wealth of variety. Neither Jason nor Laura had known where to begin and their bemused scanning had made them an obvious target for a sales assistant. And who could blame the girl for assuming they were a family or even for pointing out how tired they looked?

She could blame the assistant for the fluttering eyelashes, though, Laura thought grimly. You couldn't assume you were talking to the proud parents of a new baby and then justify flirting with the father.

'So what is it you need today?'

'Everything,' Jason said glumly.

'Sorry?' The sales assistant blinked.

'We only just got her,' Jason explained. 'Yesterday.' He raised an eyebrow at Laura. 'It *was* only yesterday, wasn't it? Feels like for ever.'

She nodded, smiling. They had arrived at Jason's house about eight a.m. Stick had already decamped, taking enough of his possessions to last a day or two. Laura had ducked home briefly later in the morning when Megan had been asleep to collect a few of her own necessities and then they had spent the rest of the day and the whole of a long night focussed on caring for the tiny person they had taken responsibility for.

Jason hadn't left things entirely to Laura. He had learned to follow the instructions on the tin and mix up formula. He just backed off when it came to holding the bottle and the baby at the same time. Laura enjoyed the feeding more than anything, so she had to admit she hadn't pushed the point. She didn't enjoy the nappy changes much but Jason had a singular talent for being either justifiably asleep or mysteriously absent whenever that task became unavoidable. She had to give him credit for his attempt to help tidy, though. Venturing into Stick's room to sleep would have been a far more memorable experience if Jason hadn't ridden shotgun to change the sheets, collect dead laundry and kick some fairly questionable magazines further under the bed.

'So she's adopted?' The sales assistant was not about to be thrown off her stride. 'That's so special! What have you called her?'

'Her name's Megan.' Laura was amused by the glance she caught. Obviously it had to be her fault that she and her partner hadn't been able to conceive a child of their own. One look at Jason had been enough to convince the assistant that there was nothing likely to be inadequate about his potency, or any method of delivery. Another approving glance provoked confusion, however.

'But…how did you find a baby with eyes just like yours?'

'We didn't,' Jason said shortly. '*She* found us. It's a long story.'

'Oh?' The girl looked eager but then flushed at Jason's hesitation. 'Sorry. It's none of my business, is it?'

'No,' Laura agreed blandly. 'Let's get on with this, shall we, Jase? I'd like to get home before Megan's due for her next feed.'

The sales assistant was losing interest. Her glance told Laura that she was a nagging wife even if she wasn't wearing a wedding ring. 'Let me know if I can help,' she said professionally. 'The cots, bassinets, prams and so forth are on the other side of the clothing section. Toys and accessories are over there. What would you like to look at first?'

'Clothes,' Laura said promptly.

'Toys,' Jason said at the same time.

Five minutes later, Laura found herself standing alone in front of a bewildering selection of clothing items. Jason was getting further away by the moment with a now animated salesgirl introducing him to the delights of baby toys. Laura saw his face split into a wide grin as a brightly coloured jester popped out of a velvety, soft-toy box. His laughter caused several heads to turn and prompted smiles from everyone. His companion's giggle was also audible and Laura tried very hard but completely failed to suppress a stab of resentment. Jealousy, even.

Did that assistant love the sound of Jason's laughter as much as she did? Did it start a delicious tingle that coalesced into something so much stronger as it knotted itself down low in her abdomen? Laura wanted to play as well. To elicit and share that laughter. So why was she holding onto an increasingly heavy baby who was starting to grizzle, trying to decide how few items of clothing it would be reasonable to purchase and whether to head for the bargain bins or the cute little outfits displayed on hangers or life-sized baby dolls like some boutique for midgets.

An older assistant appeared at her shoulder. 'They get heavy, don't they, dear? Even at this age.' Megan stopped crying for a moment and stared at the new face. 'Oh, what a poppet,' the woman cooed. 'She's just gorgeous!'

Laura smiled, feeling absurdly as though the compliment had been personal.

'Have you got a front pack? It's an ideal way to carry baby without effort and still feel nice and close.'

'No.' Laura's smile widened as a mental picture of Jason's broad chest adorned with a canvas pouch that had tiny limbs protruding from it presented itself. A faint wash of colour heated her cheeks as she realised her imagination had conjured up a bare chest above pyjama pants that looked ready to disintegrate. She cleared her throat. 'Sounds like a very good idea,' she said hurriedly. 'I need a few clothes first, though.'

'Look at these.' The woman pointed to a tiny stretchsuit, the yoke of which was adorned with hand-embroidered bumble bees. 'Isn't it darling? And it's got all the matching accessories. Hat, matinée jacket, bootees.'

Laura heard another deep rumble of laughter that could only have come from Jason as she blinked at the price tag. Megan chose that moment to start a renewed protest and Laura could no longer ignore the odour wafting from folds of blue polar fleece. It wasn't as if she was going to be paying for any of this, was it?

'I'll take the whole outfit,' she said briskly. 'Something in pink would be nice, too.'

'I don't believe this.' Jason put down his last load of purchases and shook his head slowly.

Up until yesterday this living room had been a place of refuge. Sure, the empty beer bottles tended to accumulate on the coffee-table and an unwashed plate or two might mean a less than straight passageway to the couch, but it had never bothered the men who lived there. There had been a lot of good times in this room, chilling out with some good conversation and a game of cards or winding up into a fervour of support as they watched a rugby match on television. Those good times were unimaginable right now. The living room looked as though it had become a suburban outlet for the Baby Warehouse.

'Look at all this stuff. We can't possibly need it all.'

'We certainly didn't need a whole trolley load of toys,' Laura agreed.

'And have you any *idea* how much it all cost?' Jason felt yet another echo of the shock wave the checkout girl's request had evoked, but at least the pain was starting to fade just a little. 'I had no idea babies could be so expensive. I've spent more on her clothes in one hour than I've spent on myself in the last year!'

Laura thought it might be advisable not to go into the cost of the clothing too closely. 'The bassinet was a good choice. I love the little farm animals on the ruffle.'

Jason made a low growling sound. 'She wanted me to buy a cot, would you believe? One with an adjustable mattress level that you keep putting down. Then it turns into a bed. I nearly told her we were only planning to keep the kid for a few days, not a few years.' His gaze roved over the supplies of nappies, bottles, feed and sterilising materials and the bedding, plastic bath and containers of lotion and wipes. The toys. The clothing. And yet more toys.

'I must have been mad,' he said sadly.

'Think of it as child support,' Laura said helpfully.

Jason scowled at the faintly acerbic tone. 'I'm paid up till she starts university in that case.' He watched as Laura continued her journey around the perimeter of the room, jiggling the baby, who hadn't stopped crying for more than thirty seconds at a time since they'd left the shop. The sound was really beginning to grate on raw nerve endings and Jason gritted his teeth.

No wonder Laura sounded less than sympathetic. She'd had the noise at close range while he'd spent the last half-hour unloading and arranging their purchases. She looked tired, too, and Jason experienced a moment of panic at the thought she might decide to throw in the towel and go home.

'Here…let me have a go at shutting her up.' The appreciative smile he received made the offer well worth while.

'Thanks.' Laura transferred Megan to his outstretched arms. 'I could use a break.'

'Put your feet up,' Jason said generously. 'Have a nap even.'

'What I really need is a nice long shower. My hair feels like old string.' The grimace that accompanied the tug on the ponytail made Jason look at Laura's hair consciously for the first time, and she was right. It *looked* like old string. Her glasses had smears on them and the baggy T-shirt she wore had a lot more than just smears. All in all, it wasn't an attractive package, but Jason couldn't have cared less what his new housemate looked like. He needed her. Big time.

No way could he face this alone and his best mates hadn't exactly lined up to assist, had they? Mitch had only stayed as long as it had taken to pack half his gear last night and Stick had dropped in with him to collect his CD player.

'It's a great sleep-out,' he'd informed Jason unmercifully. 'Quiet as. And Cliff's quite happy to have us stay as long as we want. He's been thinking of renting it out anyway.'

Fifteen minutes later, Jason's appreciation of Laura's efforts was waning. Just how long did it take to have a shower and wash hair? He was in trouble here. Megan's face was bright red from the effort of yelling so loudly and nothing he did seemed to make any difference. He'd tried putting her in the brand-new bassinet but she hadn't been impressed.

'Have you any idea what this thing cost?' Jason queried. 'We paid extra for those cute little sheep and pigs. You're supposed to *like* them. Here…look at this.' He picked up the soft toy jack-in-the-box and squeezed the base. The maniacally happy-looking jester flew out at close range to Megan's face. Incredibly, her howling notched up several more decibels.

Jason threw a guilty glance over his shoulder, half expecting Laura to appear and berate him for his total inadequacy in entertaining a baby. No...he was *hoping* she'd appear. He wouldn't mind being berated if he got rescued at the same time. Awkwardly, he picked up the infant again, remembering to put his hand under its head for support. Good grief, it was so *tiny*. The little head fitted into the palm of his hand and felt no bigger than a grapefruit. And it was hot, he noticed. Hardly surprising, with all that energy being expended making noise. A waft of an odour he was unfortunately becoming all too familiar with caught Jason's nostrils and he rocked the baby in his arms and stared miserably at the door.

'Come on, Laura, for God's sake,' he muttered. 'I *need* you, dammit.'

Jason looked almost as miserable as Megan sounded, Laura decided when she entered the room a few minutes later. Feeling clean and refreshed after her shower, her stress levels had declined enough for the sight to be almost amusing.

'At least it's only Megan that's howling,' she said.

'That's not funny.' Jason scowled. 'You've no idea how close I am. There's something wrong with this kid. Unless it's just because it hates *me*.'

'Let's try changing her nappy,' Laura suggested. 'That might help.' Deftly twisting her damp hair into a ponytail and securing it with a scrunchy, she then spread a towel on the floor and reached for the packet of baby wipes. 'You know, those change tables looked great. Much easier on the back to do this standing up.'

Jason deposited his shrieking bundle onto the towel with surprising gentleness. 'Hardly something you could pack up and take back to England,' he reminded her. 'We had to draw the line somewhere.'

'The bassinet isn't exactly portable either.'

'Yeah…well, I did suggest using the cardboard box if you remember.'

'Oh, I remember.' Laura chuckled as she eased Megan's legs from the stretchsuit and pulled at the nappy's plastic tags. 'I'm sure that sales assistant won't forget in a hurry either.'

Jason went a noticeable shade paler as Laura opened the nappy. 'I'm sure you need a coffee,' he said hurriedly. 'And I'd better mix up another bottle, hadn't I?'

'Mmm.' At least he'd stayed within six feet while the nappy had come off. Laura found herself smiling as she held Megan's ankles with one hand and lifted her gently to start cleaning. It was a bit like taming a wild animal, really. A little closer each time and then...bingo! She'd have him changing a nappy all by himself. It was lucky she possessed a good degree of patience. Pushing the issue would only have him diving for cover. She was getting pretty good at accomplishing this task effectively now anyway.

'There you go,' she told the baby. 'A nice clean bottom.' She picked her up for a cuddle. 'Is that better, darling? No wonder you were unhappy. I'd be unhappy if I had smelly pants, too.'

Jason cleared his throat meaningfully behind her. 'Let's not go *there*,' he warned. 'I'd appreciate it if you kept your smelly pants all to yourself. Here's the bottle.'

'Great.' Laura was pleased to hear something like Jason's usual good humour reappearing. She moved to the couch to sit down. 'Is it the right temperature?'

'I think so.' Jason held the bottle and sprinkled a few drops of milk on the inside of his wrist. Then his teeth flashed as he grinned. 'I've seen them do that on the telly.'

'And?'

'And what?'

'Does it feel hot or cold?'

'I can't feel anything.' The grin was replaced with an anxious frown. 'What's it supposed to feel like?'

'Nothing.' Laura smiled reassuringly as she held out her hand. 'If it's body temperature, like it's supposed to be, it won't feel hot *or* cold.' She tested it again. 'Perfect,' she pronounced.

Jason beamed. 'Cool. I'll see if I can get the coffee perfect as well.'

But Laura didn't touch the coffee Jason brewed. Neither did he.

'Why won't she stop crying?'

'I don't know.' Frustrated, Laura put the bottle down. 'She won't feed properly either.' They couldn't find a cure for the miserable, hiccuping sobs interspersed with some ear-splitting howls, and the continued failure made the tension the noise was creating escalate rapidly. 'I think there might be something wrong.'

'*I* told you that.'

'I thought that changing and feeding her would help. They're the first things you're supposed to try.'

'They didn't work, though, did they?' Jason said accusingly.

'Obviously not,' Laura snapped. 'Thanks, Einstein.'

'What do we do now, then?'

'I don't know.'

'What? You must have some ideas.'

'Where are *your* ideas?' Laura shot back. 'This is *your* baby, Jason Halliday. It's *your* problem. Why am I supposed to be an expert? *I've* never had a baby and, what's more, I don't intend to have one until I'm with someone who's going to be of some help as a partner.'

'I didn't *intend* to have a baby!' Jason's voice rose to something very close to a shout and Megan raised her own volume to compete. 'Jeez, Laura. I don't need this. I don't even want a bloody baby.' He turned abruptly, as though intending to walk out. 'This is a nightmare!'

Laura saw him stop after only a couple of steps, his fists clenched tightly by his sides, and she sighed heavily.

'I could ring Mrs Mack,' she offered more quietly. 'She might have some ideas.'

Jason turned. 'But then all the guys at the station will know what it's like here. They'll know I'm incompetent and I can't even babysit my own kid for a couple of days. I'll never hear the end of it.'

His look was beseeching enough to prompt another sigh from Laura. 'Have you got a thermometer in the house?'

'No. Why?'

'She feels hot. She might be running a bit of a temperature.'

Jason closed the space between them swiftly. '*I* thought that, too.' He crouched down to peer at Megan. 'She's sick, isn't she?'

'I'm not sure. It's not an obvious fever. She just feels a bit warmer than I would have expected.'

'But you're a medic. You know about this stuff.'

'Babies are tricky. Usually, by the time we get called, either the baby is obviously sick or the parents have noticed enough to be worried, so even if the baby looks fine we still transport it to hospital.'

'I'm a parent,' Jason said. 'And I'm worried. The kid's all red. It's crying all the time and it's hot.'

'It's not a colicky cry, so it's not likely to be tummy pain. She hasn't been sick, she's not coughing and she hasn't got a runny nose. Any baby is going to go red and get hot when it's crying this much.'

Laura laid her hand gently on Megan's fontanelle where it was easy to feel a pulse. She was watching the tiny chest at the same time but it was difficult to count respirations due to the hiccuping sobs. The crying was mercifully softer now. Just an ongoing sound of tired misery.

'Her breathing's fine,' Laura reported a minute later. 'Her heart rate is a little fast but that could also be because she's upset.' She shook her head. 'What bothers me is that this is the first time she hasn't accepted her bottle and calmed down. Did you mix the formula the same as last time?'

'Of course I did. This isn't *my* fault.'

'It's not *my* fault either.'

They glared at each other and Laura winced at a fresh wail from Megan. This was turning to custard. So much for that little fantasy about revealing her attractive personality to Jason.

'Let's take her to a doctor,' she suggested finally. 'At least that way we can get her temperature checked accurately.'

They spoke very little to each other during the time it took to find the local GP clinic in the phone book, make an appointment and get ready. They exchanged only the bare necessities of communication as they sat in a crowded waiting room full of sniffling toddlers and fragile-looking older people who stared accusingly at anyone making too much noise. They glared in Megan's direction on a consistent basis.

Conversation with the GP they finally saw was somewhat stilted due to the on-the-spot fabrication that Jason had agreed in advance to mind his daughter for a few days while his ex-partner had a holiday in New Zealand. It wasn't until they were home again nearly three hours later that the tension finally evaporated.

'I thought she was going to call the police and report a stolen child. I was getting sweaty palms, imagining myself being arrested.'

'It's just as well Megan is so unmistakably yours, thanks to those eyes.'

'It was really embarrassing not to be able to answer any of those questions. How would I know if the pregnancy and birth were normal?' Jason frowned. 'I *should* know. Shelley should have told me.'

'The doctor was great, giving her such a thorough checkup. She said she looks generally well cared for.'

'If she'd been well cared for she wouldn't have been left on a doorstep all night and she wouldn't have an ear infection now.'

Laura said nothing. If she told Jason that Megan had only been left outside for a matter of minutes rather than hours, she would also have to confess that the mother had been seen driving off in the company of a man and hadn't bothered with even a backward glance at her child. The implication that she wouldn't be in a hurry to collect her daughter in the next few days, and the prospect of a longer time with a miserable infant, would surely be enough to ensure Jason found a rapid escape route from this situation. And Laura didn't want that. It was too early to tell whether this could work out for any of them and she wasn't going to give up. Not yet.

'And why did the doctor say it was a shame she wasn't being breast-fed?'

'Breast-feeding gives a baby more protection against bugs. Some immunity gets passed on from the mother.'

'There you go, then,' Jason said triumphantly. 'If Shelley was a halfway decent mother she would have been breast-feeding. And she certainly wouldn't have just dumped her kid on a doorstep.'

'No.' Laura was quite happy to agree to that.

She looked down at the exhausted infant she was holding. The dose of paracetamol administered at the clinic had worked wonders and Megan was now too sleepy to finish her bottle. She had been dozing between short bursts of sucking but now felt like such a dead weight that Laura was sure she was sound asleep.

Hopefully, the GP was right and Megan would be in the fifty per cent of otitis media sufferers whose pain would settle in twenty-four hours without needing antibiotics. If it was any worse tomorrow they would have to take her back, otherwise her ears would be checked in a few days' time.

'Could you put her down in the bassinet, please, Jase?'

Jason hesitated. 'She'll wake up if I touch her. She'll start screaming again and my ears are only just starting to recover.'

'I don't think she will,' Laura said confidently. 'She's dead to the world. Come on, it's time you learned how to put your daughter to bed.'

Jason looked as rebellious as a small boy about to have a dirty face wiped but then he gave that lopsided smile that touched something deep within Laura's heart.

'OK, I'll give it a bash. But don't blame me if she wakes up. She hates me.'

Gingerly, Jason picked up the floppy baby and carried her to the bassinet.

'Put her on her side,' Laura advised. 'And then tuck the sheet over her firmly enough to make sure she doesn't roll onto her tummy.'

Jason was arranging the baby as though handling an unexploded bomb. 'Why can't she sleep on her tummy?' he asked. 'I do it all the time.'

Laura pushed back the image of Jason in those pyjama pants, sprawled prone on a mattress, with tousled blond hair and a stubble-roughened chin turned to one side. 'It's thought to be a major factor in protection against SIDS.'

'SIDS?'

'Sudden infant death syndrome. Used to be called cot death.'

Jason stared at the tiny face below him as he carefully tucked in the sheet. 'She's not going to *die*, is she?'

'Of course not.' The notion that Jason was starting to care about his child caused a wash of pleasure that was unfortunately short-lived.

'Wouldn't be a good look, would it? Handing it back to its mother if it had fallen off its perch.' Jason grinned at Laura. 'Be a bit hard to cover up my incompetence then, wouldn't it?'

'All new parents feel incompetent,' Laura said quietly. 'Babies don't come with personalised instruction manuals. We've had a sharper learning curve than most, what with her unexpected arrival and her being unwell, but we're doing OK.'

Jason simply nodded and Laura hugged the fact he hadn't questioned their partnership as unexpected parents for Megan. It wasn't a lot but it was enough to be going on with and the silence in the room seemed to herald a peacefulness that bordered on contentment. Almost.

'I am *so* hungry,' Laura had to confess. 'Did you notice we missed lunch?'

'Now that you mention it.' Jason looked at his watch and his eyes widened. 'We've almost missed dinner as well. I can't believe I've gone so long without food. I hadn't even been thinking about it.'

'You had other things to think about.'

'Yeah. Did you see all those old fogies giving us the death glare in that waiting room?'

Laura nodded, smiling.

'You would have thought it was *us* making the noise, not our kid.' Jason sounded affronted now.

Laura nodded her agreement and the glance they shared was one of understanding. The elderly patients had forgotten or never known what it was like to care for a new baby. Laura and Jason knew.

Our kid. Laura's smile widened and Jason smiled right back at her.

'I could kill for some of Mrs Mack's bacon and eggs right now.'

'Me, too.'

'And a beer.' Jason raised an eyebrow. 'I s'pose you'd rather have wine or something?'

'No. I like beer.'

'Really?' Jason gave Laura an assessing glance and then his smile widened. 'Cool. I've got some in the fridge.'

'Great.'

'There's some bacon and eggs there as well, I think. Unless Stick ate them when I wasn't looking. Did you know I can cook?'

'No. You seemed to know where all the take-away shops in the area were when you went out last night.'

Jason's chin lifted at the challenge. 'Stay right where you are,' he ordered. 'You're in for a treat, babe.'

It *was* a treat. Crispy bacon, perfectly cooked eggs and thick slices of soft buttered bread all washed down with icy-cold lager. Megan slept on...and on. They did the dishes, sterilised bottles, made up the night feeds and sorted all the new baby purchases into tidied positions. And still Megan slept.

'Do you think she's all right?' Jason peered into the bassinet. 'I can't tell if she's even breathing.'

'She's fine,' Laura told him. 'She's got a lot of sleep to catch up on.'

'She's not the only one.' Jason flopped onto the couch beside Laura and yawned hugely. 'Shall I put the bassinet in your room, then?'

Laura cleared her throat. 'I was thinking it could go in *your* room.'

They eyed each other warily.

'Maybe...' Jason sounded hopeful. 'We could leave it in here and take turns getting up?'

'Megan's not an ''it'', Jason.'

'I was talking about the bassinet.'

'Oh...OK.' Laura let that one pass. 'All right. Sounds fair to me. Who's going to get up first?'

'Um.' Jason seemed to have found something fascinating to look at on the ceiling. Laura tilted her head back as well.

'Whose baby is this, Jason Halliday?'

'She loves *you*.'

'She'll love you, too, if you give her half a chance. Feeding her will make a big difference.'

'I don't know *how* to feed her.'

'You just hold the bottle. She'll do the rest.'

Jason was silent.

'How 'bout we do the first night feed to-gether?' Laura suggested generously. 'You can feed her and I'll change her nappy.'

'Sounds like a plan.'

'Then you can do the next one by yourself.'

'But…' Jason turned his head and caught Laura's expression at close range. 'Oh, all right. I'll give it a bash.'

'Good for you.'

Jason sighed heavily a moment later and Laura had to smile.

'You're finding this pretty rough, aren't you?'

'It's a nightmare,' Jason admitted.

'So you never wanted a family, then?'

'Of course I did. Do,' Jason corrected himself. 'I just planned on being in love with the mother of my kids. Planned on planning the kids for that matter.' He sighed again. 'Shelley Bates certainly wouldn't have been on the list of potential candidates.'

'You weren't in love with her, then?'

'I've never been in love.'

'Oh, come on!' Laura's eyes snapped open. 'You're permanently in love. It's just that the object of your affections gets updated at regular intervals.'

'Of course it does. That's because I've never found what I'm looking for. If I was really in love I wouldn't have to keep looking, would I?'

Laura's heart skipped a beat. 'What are you looking for, Jase?'

'I wish I knew.'

'Maybe you're using the wrong search engine.'

'Don't think so. I know what I like.'

'Which is?'

'Well, they have to be great-looking.'

Laura's snort summed up what she thought of that criterion.

'Hey, it's not just the looks I go for. I'm not *that* shallow. I always test out intelligence with an in-depth discussion on current world politics.'

Laura thought of the yellow bikini-clad bimbo. 'Really?'

'No.' Jason grinned and Laura shook her head even as she chuckled.

'There you go. You *are* shallow.'

'No, I'm not,' Jason protested. 'There's more to my girlfriends than the way they look.'

'Like what?'

'They have to be fun to be with,' Jason said seriously. 'Adventurous. And at least reasonably intelligent. Maybe that's why they never last,' he added sadly. 'Even the most promising ones get boring.'

'What's the longest relationship you've had, Jase?'

'Twelve months. How 'bout you?'

'I lived with someone for two years.'

'Didn't work out, then?'

'No.'

'Got boring, huh?'

'You could say that. John just wanted someone to cook and clean and devote themselves to making him happy.'

Jason grinned. 'Works for me.'

Laura aimed a punch at his upper arm. 'I was joking,' he protested, rubbing his arm.

'It's not funny,' Laura told him primly. 'And I'm never going to get trapped like that again. In my book, loving someone doesn't mean you get to control or take advantage of them.'

Jason sat up. 'Hey, I hope you don't think *I'm* taking advantage of you. You did offer to help look after Megan, you know.'

'I know,' Laura confirmed.

'Why did you?' Jason rested his head on the back of the couch again. 'All my other mates have done a very effective job of disappearing into the woodwork. I might just have a few words to them about that.'

'Maybe I'm just a nice person,' Laura said lightly. She yawned and closed her eyes. 'Right now, I'm a very tired person. I haven't had any sleep worth mentioning for rather a long time.'

Jason could sense the moment Laura fell asleep only minutes later. Very slowly, her head tipped sideways until it was resting on his shoulder. He turned his head, intending to suggest she wake up enough to go and lie down properly, but something stopped him.

Maybe it was the softness of her hair brushing his cheek or the fresh scent of some kind of flowery shampoo she had used. Or maybe it was just the good feeling it gave him that she trusted him enough to use his shoulder as a pillow. Or the fact that she had fallen asleep from exhaustion due to helping him with a task he'd have had no hope of managing on his own. He'd never done anything he could think of that might have inspired such a generous response on Laura's part.

She had been telling the truth even if it had been intended as a joke. Laura Green *was* a nice person.

A very nice person indeed.

CHAPTER FOUR

'THREE-TEN Robbins Avenue. Three-one-zero.'

The elastic braces on Jason's over-trousers were still dangling as he reached for his coat and helmet.

'Smoke seen to be pouring from rear of house.' The calm voice of the dispatch officer managed to override the insistent blare of the alarm sounding through the loudspeaker system of Inglewood station. 'Multiple calls.'

Jason caught Stick's gaze and grinned at the anticipation in his colleague's face. Multiple calls to the emergency response control centre invariably meant that the job was genuine rather than a false alarm or prank call. He was feeling pretty excited himself. This was the first callout for Green Watch day shift and it had happened within minutes of arriving for work.

After four days of the nightmare his personal life had become, this felt like the clock was being wound back. *This* was his real life.

He could forget about Megan and Laura and even the nebulous spectre of Shelley Bates and any upcoming confrontation.

Except that his Green Watch colleagues weren't about to allow him any respite no matter how urgent the callout. Jason was on the back bench seat of the passenger compartment, sitting beside Stick. Cliff was navigating in the front passenger seat and Bruce was driving. Thirteen tons of fire appliance was soon gathering speed, siren on and beacons flashing. Jason pulled his braces into place and managed to shove his arms into his coat sleeves despite the limited space available to manoeuvre.

'Put your safety belt on, Dad.'

'Give it a rest, Stick.' The ribbing had started well before the official shift change. Laura had taken it with good humour. In fact, Jason had the weird impression that she hadn't even minded being addressed as 'Mummy'. And Mrs McKendry might have pretended to be offended by Stick and Mitch deciding to call her 'Granny M.' but it had been quite obvious she couldn't wait to whisk the bassinet into a quiet corner of 'her' kitchen.

Jason clicked his lap belt into place just in time to prevent ending up on Stick's lap as Bruce negotiated a sharp corner.

'Unit 962—are you responding?'

'Affirmative.' Cliff looked up from his map to check that the appropriate button on the radio console had been activated. The response button was still flashing, which indicated the signal hadn't gone through, so he pushed it again.

'Person thought to be trapped. Back-up has been dispatched from Central Station. Ambos are also on their way.'

'Won't be our guys,' Bruce said. 'They got sent out to someone who was unconscious or something.'

Jason looked ahead over Bruce's shoulder as the air horn added considerably to the noise they were making. Drivers at the intersection they were entering hurriedly jammed on their brakes or pulled to the side of the road.

'Take the next right and head up to the top of the hill,' Cliff advised Bruce. 'Then take a left into Kowhai Drive.'

'I wonder who's trapped.' Stick said. 'Hope it's not another kid.'

Too many young lives had been lost in house fires around the country recently and it was an experience all fire officers dreaded having to deal with. Dwelling on the darker side of what the job entailed was never tolerated for long, however. Especially with this particular crew.

'We'll send Jase in to look after it, if it is.' Cliff turned to grin over his shoulder. 'He's the expert now.'

'Amazing that he's lasted four days.' Bruce had to shout to be heard as he leaned on the horn at another intersection. 'Have you learned how to change a nappy yet, mate?'

'He's bloody lucky he's got Laura there to help.'

'Yeah. Good old Laura. You wouldn't think it to look at her but she's a bit of a star, isn't she?'

'She probably wouldn't look half bad either if she lost a bit of weight.'

'She's not fat.' Jason was stung out of trying to ignore the conversation.

'She's not exactly skinny,' Stick declared.

Cliff was grinning again. 'I like a few curves,' he said. 'Makes them a bit more cuddly, doesn't it, Jase?'

'I wouldn't know.'

'Pull the other one! You've had a female alone in the house with you for four days and you haven't tried it on?'

'Of course not.' Jason was more than affronted this time. 'This is *Laura* we're talking about.'

The nods of the surrounding men signalled an end to that ridiculous line of discussion, and perversely Jason felt irritated at their ready agreement. He might not find her physically attractive himself but what was so wrong with Laura? She was a nice person. She deserved to be judged on something other than her appearance.

'Babies have that effect on any relationship anyway,' Cliff told his mates. 'I remember it only too well. In fact, things were never the same in that department after the first one came along. Liz was always "too tired".'

'I'm not having a relationship with Laura.' Jason felt obliged to spell it out. 'She's just helping me out, which is more than you lot have done.'

'*We* don't fancy you, mate.' The shout of laughter Stick's comment generated was loudly appreciative.

'Neither does Laura, so give it a rest, for God's sake. How close are we now, Cliff?'

Bruce had to slow the truck to take the turn into Kowhai Drive. Then he put his foot down for a long, straight stretch.

'Have you heard from the kid's mother yet?'

'Nah.' Jason shook his head. 'Not a peep.'

'Maybe she's done a runner.'

'She won't get far. I rang a buddy in the police department and he made a few enquiries off the record. I'll get notified if she's trying to leave the country.'

'Maybe she's left already.'

Jason shook his head again. 'We checked. She arrived in Auckland five days ago from London.'

'The kid actually looked quite happy when you arrived this morning, Jase.' Stick elbowed his colleague. 'Have you got it on drugs or something?'

Bruce shot a quick glance into the back seat. 'Maybe it knows Granny M. is going to be in charge of it today.'

Referring to a child as an 'it' was really quite annoying, Jason decided. But hadn't he been doing that himself until rather recently?

'Robbins Avenue is the next on the right,' Cliff informed Bruce.

'I can smell smoke,' Stick called.

He and Jason both unclipped their safety belts and slipped their arms through the straps that would hold the tanks of air on their backs.

'And thar she blows.' They could all see the billowing cloud of smoke as they turned the next corner.

Jason put his breathing apparatus mask over his face, adjusted the straps and then pulled his helmet forward and lowered the visor. By the time he and Stick dismounted from the step on the side of the fire truck they were ready to unroll a hose and move towards whatever area their officer, Cliff, deemed the most effective place to start containing this house fire.

A small crowd of people had gathered on the footpath, many still wearing nightwear and dressing-gowns. A distraught-looking woman holding a baby, with an older child clinging to her legs and crying with terror, was the focus of attention. A man with a garden hose could be seen making a futile effort to control flames licking through the top of a bay window to-wards the iron roof of the old weatherboard house.

As driver and pump operator, Bruce was responsible for setting up the water connection. A standpipe was fitted into the nearby hydrant with the key and bar beside it. Feeder hoses connected the standpipe to the pump appliance and Jason and Stick took the delivery hose from the truck towards the house. Cliff was directing the operation, sizing up the scene and safety considerations, issuing instructions and gathering any available information from the witnesses.

'One adult escaped and managed to get two kids out,' he informed Stick and Jason. 'There's a three-year-old somewhere in the house.'

Jason swore under his breath. 'Any idea where?'

'No. She disappeared when the mother was carrying the baby and dragging the older one out.'

Another fire appliance was pulling up now and an ambulance wasn't far behind, but Jason barely registered their arrival. He used his boot to kick open the front door of the house. He pulled the handle on the branch of the hose back to open the water flow enough to send a controlled spray, which he aimed towards the ceiling of the smoke-filled hallway.

The water vaporised instantly in the heat, and steam billowed downwards. Waiting only a second or two for the steam to dissipate, Jason and Stick walked into the house.

Another burst of water cooled the top layer of smoke and the firefighters threw themselves down to avoid the burning steam. Jason could feel the heat on his ears, which were the only unprotected areas of skin on his body.

A window exploded somewhere further away in the house and he could hear the faint shouts of another fire crew setting up a second high-pressure delivery system. The sound of his own rapid breathing inside his mask was louder.

Jason pushed himself to his feet and directed a new spray of water towards the ceiling. Cooling the top layer was intended to prevent the hot gas igniting and creating a dangerous flash over and transition from a localised fire to total involvement that could trap the firefighters. He wasn't going to slow their progress any more than was absolutely necessary, however. Somewhere in here was a child and if she hadn't already succumbed to the fire or smoke inhalation, he was going to find and rescue her.

One bedroom was virtually intact but there was no sign of a child through the drifts of smoke. Handing control of the hose nozzle to Stick, Jason wrenched open the wardrobe door and swept the beam from his high-powered torch under the bed. Nothing.

The smoke in the next bedroom was thick enough to kill anybody trying to breathe it, but the area below knee level was still relatively clear. The sight of scattered toys on the floor was an unnecessary reminder of how urgent this task was, and Jason clung onto the hope that the kid had crawled in any attempt to escape and would therefore have had a supply of oxygen for longer. He shook his head, giving Stick a thumbs-down signal before moving rapidly out of the second bedroom.

Another crew was now entering the house from the other side. Between bursts of water and avoiding injury from the steam, Jason veered away from the kitchen that was the most likely starting point of this fire as a charred beam snapped and sent a shower of debris into the area. A sitting room adjoined the kitchen, but that was closer to the back-up crew. Jason turned into another short hallway.

The bathroom was clear. So was another bedroom. That left only the laundry at the end of the hallway and there was no space for a child to hide there. A washing machine, a tumble dryer and a hamper full of dirty laundry filled all the available space. Jason turned again but then paused as he reoriented himself in the eerie darkness caused by the smoke and tried to clear extraneous messages bombarding his brain.

Logically, he should go and check the sitting room and kitchen with the new crew and then use them to help double-check the rest of the house, but as he shut his eyes for a second, Jason knew he wasn't going to do that. He had been in this kind of space often enough to have learned to trust his instinct. That gut feeling that he had missed something closer to hand had been strong enough to make him pause and he couldn't afford to ignore it.

Signalling to Stick, Jason turned back, passed the bathroom and third bedroom without a second glance and, after Stick had given the ceiling a good spray of water, stepped into the laundry again. He opened the door of the tumble dryer and smoke rushed in to dull the shine of the empty drum. He pulled up the lid of the wicker laundry basket again. This time he also pulled at the dirty linen it contained. Two towels, some baby stretchsuits and several bibs came flying out to land in the puddles of water accumulating on the floor.

He'd have to give Stick a hard time later about the amount of water he was using, Jason thought fleetingly. The aim of good firefighting was to use only as much as it took to make steam. That way, no water damage would be added to whatever could be saved from destruction by flames and smoke.

His gloved hand caught the corner of a sheet. It seemed to have become tangled with other linen. Jason pulled harder and then realised that no amount of dirty washing could weigh that much. He reached in more carefully, using his torch to illuminate the bottom of the large, square basket.

And there she was. A tiny child, curled into what looked like a foetal position, cushioned on more crumpled sheets and clothes. Jason hit the button on the alarm pack attached to his sleeve to summon urgent assistance. He dropped his torch and lifted the child into his arms. Fire officers responding to the loud beep of the alarm guided him through the quickest route out of the house, via the sitting room and a set of French doors leading to a verandah. An ambulance crew was waiting and Jason experienced a wave of relief at seeing the familiar faces of Tim and Laura.

'Put her down on the blanket, mate.' Tim couldn't recognise Jason under his full protective gear. Jason put the little girl down as gently as he could. Did Laura have any idea who had delivered their patient? Or any idea how horrific he was finding this? The mother of the child obviously did. Jason could see her near the first ambulance that had arrived on scene. The blanket covering her thin nightdress was coming adrift, her oxygen mask had been ripped clear and the two ambulance officers caring for her and the other two children were both fully occupied, trying to restrain the woman from rushing into the resuscitation area that Tim and Laura had set up.

Jason could understand her anguish. The thought that he might have just carried a dead child in his arms was unbearable. He pulled off his respirator, turned off his breathing apparatus and then stayed, rooted to the spot, his eyes glued on the paramedics as they set to work on the child. *Please*, he found himself trying to tell Laura telepathically. *Do something. Save this kid.*

'Respiratory arrest.' Tim had his head very close to the child's face and one hand was now resting on her neck. 'No pulse.'

Laura was ripping open the child's pyjama jacket. It was made of pale pink fabric and decorated with little yellow ducks, rather like the ones on Megan's blanket. Jason found he had to swallow a painful lump in his throat. This kid had a father. How would he be feeling if he were standing here right now? He focussed on Laura's actions. She clearly knew what she was doing, hooking up electrodes and pushing buttons on the life pack with deft, rapid movements. Jason sent another silent prayer in her direction. *You can do it, Laura. Save her. Please.*

A line appeared on the screen of the life pack. A wiggle that even Jason knew was a long way from normal, but Laura actually looked excited.

'She's in VF,' she told Tim.

'Really?' Tim sounded amazed. 'Great.' He inflated the small lungs again carefully with the bag mask. 'We might be in with a chance here, then.'

Jason caught the shred of hope and clung to it. A chance was good. A hell of a lot better than seeing the team shaking their heads sadly or packing up anyway.

'Does anyone know how old she is?' Laura was opening a side pocket on the life pack's case, pulling out some paddles with small, silver discs on them.

'She's three.' Jason didn't recognise the strange hoarseness of his own voice.

'Age times two plus eight,' Tim said.

'Yeah, but she's tiny,' Laura responded. 'I'd put her weight at more like ten kilos.' She turned a button on the life pack. 'I'll shock at twenty kilojoules initially.'

'OK.' Tim had inserted a plastic airway into the child's mouth. The bag mask unit was connected to an oxygen cylinder. He reached for another pack and unrolled it. 'I'll get ready to intubate.'

'We'll need IV access as well.' Laura slapped some orange pads onto the small chest. 'Everyone clear,' she advised as she positioned the paddles.

'Clear,' Tim responded.

The child didn't give a dramatic jerk the way Jason had witnessed in some cardiac arrest situations. In fact, it didn't look like those little paddles had done much at all. Maybe they should use bigger ones. There had to be some way of saving this kid. She was only three, for God's sake. Would Megan still be this tiny when she was three? The thought hit Jason like a brick and the desire to protect his own child from anything like this was unexpectedly fierce. It was followed swiftly by an equally unexpected urge to get back to Inglewood station as quickly as possible and check that Megan was OK.

'Still in VF,' Laura announced. 'Shocking again at twenty kilojoules.'

Jason shut his eyes. This wasn't working and he didn't want to see what was happening to the poor kid. He was going to make damned sure nothing like this ever happened to Megan.

'Stand clear,' Laura ordered.

'Clear,' Tim responded instantly.

Except he wasn't going to be in any position to protect Megan, was he? Any day now he'd be handing the kid back to its mother, coming to some hopefully amicable financial arrangements, and then the baby would be whisked out of his life and back to the other side of the world. Which was exactly what he wanted.

Wasn't it?

'We've got sinus rhythm.' Laura sounded calm but Jason could feel the excitement in the air crank up several notches. Sinus rhythm was good. In fact, it was normal, wasn't it?

'Still not breathing,' Tim said. He pressed the bag again gently and they all watched the tiny chest rise and fall.

'Still in sinus rhythm.' Laura seemed to be able to have one eye on the life-pack screen even as her hands were fully occupied ripping open packages and then inserting a needle into the child's arm. Jason had never seen her working in such a tense situation before. This was life-and-death stuff and Laura looked completely in control. She was calm and clearly very, very competent. Jason suddenly felt rather proud to know this woman. Laura Green wasn't just a very nice person. She was also very clever.

'Spontaneous breath.' Tim looked up at Laura and Jason could see the triumph in his glance. It was clouded by something still grim, however. 'How long did that take?'

'It's less than a minute since we got a pulse,' Laura responded. 'But we don't know how long she was in arrest for.'

'Can't have been long if she was still in VF,' Tim said. 'We might be lucky.'

'We'll soon find out.' Laura nodded. 'Respiratory rate is up to about sixteen now. Get the pulse oximeter on, Tim, and let's see what her saturation levels are. We should get the mother over here, too, and fill her in with what's happening.'

Activity around the paramedic crew had continued. Jason checked his watch, astonished to find that only minutes had passed. It seemed longer. The house fire was now well under control. There were no visible flames and the thick smell of smoke in the air was dissipating already. He could see fire officers inside, damping down hot spots, but others were beginning to clean up. Hoses were being rolled away and water connections closed off. Jason knew he should move off and start helping with the clean-up but he stayed where he was. Hell, a life had been saved here, and he was part of the team. He had to know what the outcome was. Just like the kid's mother did.

'*Vicky!* Oh, my God…is she going to be all right?'

'She's breathing on her own,' Laura told the mother. 'And her heart's beating normally again.' She put a comforting hand on the arm of the woman, who looked no older than herself. 'What we don't know at this stage is how long she was low on oxygen for. She's still a very sick little girl.'

'Oh, no…' Vicky's mother sagged against the other ambulance officer as she sobbed. 'She's still going to die, isn't she?'

'No—she's not.' Jason could see a look of alarm on Laura's face as he made the confident statement but he had just seen something that filled him with elation. 'Look!'

They all looked down. A small arm was moving, then the head. And the child was making a sound. A cough? A cry? Tim pulled the airway protection device from the child's mouth just as the eyes opened. And then the miracle happened. The tiny girl looked at all the faces looming over her and saw her mother. Two small arms, one trailing an IV line, were held up with mute appeal.

'She recognises Mum.' Tim had a broad grin on his face.

'Can I pick her up? *Please?*'

'Of course.' Laura crouched again to adjust wires and help lift the child. 'You can hold her in the ambulance and we'll take you into hospital together.'

'She's going to be all right, though, isn't she?' Tears were streaming down the young mother's face as she gathered the child into her arms. 'Not...brain damaged or anything?'

Laura seemed to be hesitating as she grabbed the IV line to prevent it tangling as Vicky wrapped her arms around her mother's neck.

'Mum-*meee*...'

They all heard the child's faint but unmistakable cry. Laura's smile wobbled around the edges.

'I think she's going to be fine,' she said. 'But we still need to get her into hospital straight away.'

'Wait!' The mother turned as she was being ushered up the steps into the back of the ambulance. 'Who was it who found her? Where was she?'

Jason stepped forward.

'She was in the laundry basket,' he told her. 'Underneath the washing.'

Vicky's mother was laughing and crying at the same time. 'That's one of her favourite places for hide and seek,' she said brokenly, 'but I would never have thought of looking there.'

'It might have saved her,' Jason said. 'All the clothes would have protected her from the smoke.'

'*You* saved her. I...I don't know how to thank you.'

'These guys did a lot more than I did,' Jason waved his arm towards the ambulance crew, appalled to feel that painful lump back in this throat. This time it was made worse by an ominous prickling sensation in the corners of his eyes. 'You go with them now,' he added gruffly. 'I've got work I should be doing.'

Any assistance with the clean-up operations had to wait another minute or two, however. Jason watched both ambulances leaving the scene as he pulled himself back together. This was ridiculous. OK, they had saved the kid's life and that was a thrill, but he'd seen young victims of house fires before. Some of those had been lucky as well, but he'd never experienced such an emotional response to any job as he had this morning.

It wasn't until he was back on station and everything was tidy enough to let the crew take time out for a well-deserved break that Jason started to feel settled again. And that was crazy. Who would have thought it would help, having a baby shoved into his arms, along with a bottle of milk and instructions to feed his daughter *before* he fed himself any of Mrs M.'s delicious double-chocolate muffins, still warm from the oven.

But help it did. She was warm and heavy and felt…alive. Stick's eyebrows shot up as Jason tucked the baby into the crook of his arm and started feeding her without any drama. Jason tried to sound nonchalant.

'It's not as tough as it looks. You just hold the bottle and she does the rest.'

Stick watched the baby's vigorous sucking, the big eyes that were fastened intently on her father's face and the miniature hand that looked as though it was trying to help hold the bottle.

'She's actually kinda cute, isn't she?'

'You won't say that when her nappy needs changing, believe me. You should have seen what I had to deal with last night.'

Stick's grimace was sympathetic. 'Gross, huh?'

'Worse than gross, mate. It looked like—'

'Do you mind?' Bruce was reaching for a second muffin. 'We're trying to eat here.'

'Save some for me, ' Jason warned. He looked down at Megan. 'Hurry up,' he urged. 'It's my turn.'

'Bet you say that to all the girls.' Stick grinned.

Jason had to join in the burst of laughter. Yes, he felt much better. He could still have a good time with his mates even if he was holding a baby and a bottle.

And couldn't even reach the chocolate muffins.

CHAPTER FIVE

THE surprise was enough to stop her in her tracks.

Fortunately, Laura recovered swiftly enough to prevent Tim bowling her over as he followed her into the commonroom. It wasn't the first time she had seen Jason feeding his daughter after all. They had sorted that one out the night after the visit to the doctor. It was just the first time she'd seen him looking as though he was enjoying the duty. He was actually laughing.

'What's the joke?' Laura reached for the cup of coffee Mrs McKendry miraculously had ready for her and smiled her thanks.

'Don't ask,' Bruce advised.

'How's Vicky doing?' Jason's query was casual but Laura could see how important her answer was when she caught his gaze.

'She's going to be fine.' It was Tim who answered, sitting down at the table and reaching for a muffin. 'She's one lucky kid.'

Laura eyed the muffins but decided against having one. 'She sure is. I didn't think we had a chance to start with.' She turned to Tim. 'As soon as you said there was no pulse, I thought that was it.'

'I couldn't believe it when you found she was in VF.' Tim was grinning around the edges of his muffin. 'Great job, huh?'

Laura found Jason was still staring as he listened intently. 'When a child has a cardiac arrest, it usually follows a respiratory arrest,' she explained. 'And by then the damage from no oxygen is irreversible.'

Tim was nodding. 'Last case like that I had, we managed to resuscitate this toddler after he'd choked on a button or something. We got him back but they had to turn the life support off two days later.'

'Normally, they go straight into asystole instead of VF as well,' Laura said. 'So you can't just shock them back into a normal rhythm. That's why we got excited when we saw what we were dealing with.'

'What's VF?' Stick queried.

'Ventricular fibrillation,' Laura explained. 'The ventricles are the more important chambers of the heart. In a normal rhythm they're contracting strongly and pumping the blood out to the rest of the body. Fibrillating means that there's a very uncoordinated movement in the heart muscle and it's ineffective for pumping.'

'Whatever.' Stick wasn't interested in improving his anatomical knowledge.

'How come you got there so fast?' Bruce asked. 'I thought you got sent out to some unconscious person.'

'He was asleep.' Tim grinned. 'And rather drunk.'

'That was lucky,' Stick told them. 'You guys were awesome at the fire from what we heard. Jase hasn't stopped talking about it.'

'It was just the first time I've hung around to watch.' Jason's ears had gone pink enough for Laura to realise he was embarrassed. 'It was pretty impressive.' He was avoiding Laura's gaze and she dropped her own to her coffee-mug. Heavens, had he been impressed by *her*?

'It was more than that,' Bruce said. 'You should have seen him, Laura. He was standing there, all misty-eyed, watching you drive the kid off to the hospital.'

'I was not,' Jason protested. Then he gazed down at Megan and adjusted the tilt of the bottle he was holding. 'OK,' he admitted. His ears were an even brighter shade of pink now. 'It *did* get to me. Dunno why.'

'It's because it was a kid,' Bruce suggested.

'I've rescued kids before.'

'It's because you're a dad now,' Cliff stated. 'It changes things.'

'Nah. Why should it?'

'It's true.' Laura nodded at Cliff. 'I've seen the way friends change once they've had a baby. It changes your whole perspective.'

'Sure does. You get a connection to other people that makes you more…human, I guess. Or less selfish or something.'

'Less selfish is good.' Jason was glaring at Bruce. 'I hope you're not really intending to eat that last muffin. You've had two already.'

'What about the rest of the family?' Cliff asked Laura. 'Were they all OK?'

'They all needed treatment for smoke inhalation and they're keeping Vicky in for observation, but I imagine they'll all be able to be discharged tomorrow.'

'Did they say anything about what might have caused the fire?' Bruce looked at the last muffin, looked at Jason and then sighed in defeat. 'I didn't get a chance to interview the mother.'

'Apparently the older boy was trying to make breakfast. The toaster jammed and the curtains caught fire. His mother had taken the baby back to bed to feed him and she'd fallen asleep again. It was the neighbour who raised the alarm and woke her up.'

'Where was the father?'

'Who knows?' Tim responded. 'He walked out when the last baby was born ten months ago.'

'Bastard.'

There was a tiny silence after Jason's expletive. Then Bruce raised an eyebrow. 'So you wouldn't walk out on your kid, then, Jase?'

'No, I bloody wouldn't.'

'So are you going to go back to England with this Shelley, then?' Stick sounded worried.

'No. Of course not.'

'Maybe she'll want to stay here,' Stick suggested morosely. 'Maybe she'll want to marry her kid's father.'

'Would you do that, Jase?' Cliff gave his younger colleague a speculative glance.

'Hey, I'm not going to *marry* someone I don't love. I'm not that stupid. But I'm not going to desert my kid either.'

Laura wasn't the only one to sense the internal conflict but she was quite sure she was more bothered than anyone else in the room. What if Mrs McKendry's impressions had been wrong and this Shelley *was* intending to come back? Whatever intentions Megan's mother had, she had laid a very solid base by leaving the baby in Jason's care. It had been a clever move. Jason was a very decent bloke. He was starting to care about Megan, whether he realised it or not. His daughter could prove to be a very powerful bargaining tool if this Shelley Bates was planning to manipulate him into doing more than babysitting.

'Maybe you should go for custody, then,' Bruce advised.

Laura bit her lip. If Jason did that, he would need someone to help—full time. An even wilder thought occurred. If Jason married *her*, he would be safe from whatever manipulative plans Megan's mother might have. She shook her head imperceptibly to chase the thought back to where it belonged, which was precisely nowhere. As if!

'Yeah.' Cliff was backing Bruce up. 'She's already proved herself to be an unfit mother by dumping the kid on a doorstep. You'd be in with a good chance of winning, mate.'

Jason was looking positively alarmed. 'I didn't say I wanted to *keep* it,' he said hurriedly. '*Her*,' he amended just as hastily.

They all heard the disapproving sniff that came from the kitchen.

'I'll pay maintenance,' Jason said defensively. 'And send her birthday presents and stuff. If she *is* living overseas, she can come and visit me for holidays when she's a bit older.'

'Like in ten years' time?' Stick offered.

Jason's wide grin was relieved. 'Works for me, mate.'

The sniff was at much closer range this time. 'Has that bairn finished her bottle?'

Jason held it up. 'Every drop, Mackie. See?'

'Time you changed her nappy, then.'

Jason caught Laura's eye at the same instant her pager sounded. She grinned. 'Sorry, buddy. You're on your own this time.'

Tempted to grab that last muffin on her way out the door, Laura was pleased when she managed to dismiss the urge. Whether it was the lack of sleep or the stress of caring for a baby that was doing it, her clothes felt slightly looser than they had four days ago. It wasn't a huge difference but she rather liked the sensation of comfort it gave her.

The call was a priority one response to a 'shortness of breath' case.

'What do you reckon?' Tim queried as they cleared the garage. 'Asthma, pneumonia or heart failure?'

Laura flicked the switch to start the beacons flashing. Her finger was poised over the control for the siren but the road was quiet enough for it not to be necessary yet. 'Could be an acute myocardial infarction,' she offered. 'That can make you a bit short of breath.'

'So can smoke inhalation.' Tim pulled the map from the pocket between the gear shift and the dashboard. 'We were lucky with that kid this morning, weren't we?'

'I'll say.' Laura smiled. A job like that always reminded her how much she loved this career. It more than made up for all the time and effort spent on less than genuine cases.

Like the one they were dispatched to as their final call for the day. The 'traumatic injury' turned out to be back pain that the grossly overweight, middle-aged woman had been suffering from for ten years.

'Has it got any worse suddenly today?' Laura asked.

'No. And it hasn't got any better either.'

'Who called for the ambulance?' A thin, tired-looking man had opened the door to them and Laura was assuming he was their patient's husband.

'*I* did,' the woman said belligerently. 'What am I supposed to have done? The doctor's bloody useless. I rang him and he said to take some pills. I'm a bloody walking pharmacy as it is. I rattle when I walk. I'm fed up to the back teeth with taking bloody pills.'

'What medications are you on?' Laura was beginning to understand why the man was so quiet and weary. She'd only been in the room for two minutes and she was more than ready to escape. Tim was having trouble getting the Velcro on the extra-large size of blood-pressure cuff to meet around her upper arm. He was also carefully avoiding Laura's eye and she suspected he was having difficulty keeping a straight face.

'Ow!' The oversized arm was moved enough to displace the disc of Tim's stethoscope. 'That *hurts*.'

'It'll only be tight for a few seconds,' Tim responded patiently. 'Try and keep still.'

Laura caught the gaze of the man. 'Has your wife got a list of her medications anywhere?'

'She's not my wife, she's my mother.'

'Sorry.' Maybe living with the woman had aged him rapidly. Laura was feeling older by the minute. If the squeeze of a blood-pressure cuff was enough to elicit such an agonised response, the back pain was probably no more than a mild ache. Her impression that they were wasting their time strengthened as she read the list of medications.

'So you're taking pills for your high blood pressure, high cholesterol, diabetes, airways disease, depression, weight control, constipation and pain—is that right?'

'Isn't that enough?'

Laura stepped over an overflowing dinner plate that was being used as an ashtray. 'When was the last time you were in hospital, Mrs Pearce?'

'Two weeks ago.'

'And what was that for?'

'Stomach pain. Something terrible it was. I was in bloody agony.'

'What did they say at the hospital?'

'They gave me six enemas. *Six!* If they knew what they were doing it should have only taken one. They're all useless, the whole lot of them, and I told them so.'

'Did they say anything else?'

Mrs Pearce's son sighed heavily. 'They told Mum to stop smoking, lose some weight and start getting some exercise.'

'And *I* told them, if they could do what they're supposed to be doing and fix me up then I might be able to start doing some bloody exercise. What do they expect? Some sort of miracle? I have enough trouble getting out of my chair and *they* seem to think I can go trotting around the block at the drop of a bloody hat.'

Tim had finished taking basic vital signs and filling in the paperwork. 'There's no real need for you to go to the hospital right now, Mrs Pearce. You'll end up waiting for hours and then being sent home, probably with exactly the same advice you were given last time. Is that what you want?'

'I want to get fixed up. I'm not going to get anywhere if I just sit at home and put up with it, am I?' She glared at Tim. 'It's the squeaky door that gets the bloody oil.'

'Fine.' Laura wanted to get this job over with. 'But you'll need to walk out to the ambulance for us, Mrs Pearce.'

'I can't move. My back's too sore.'

Laura caught Tim's eye. Their patient weighed at least a hundred and forty kilograms. They would be lucky to fit Mrs Pearce onto a stretcher with both sides down, and a scoop stretcher would probably buckle under the strain.

'We'll need to get some help to move you, in that case,' Tim said tactfully. 'That might take a while.'

'Are you saying I'm fat?'

Yes! Laura wanted to shout. *You are grossly overweight and we're not going to wreck our backs when you're probably perfectly capable of walking. You're wasting our time and we're not going to be popular when we hand you over to emergency department staff who have far better things to do than spend time on someone who has no intention of taking re-*

sponsibility for their own health. Instead, she smiled, albeit somewhat grimly.

'You have a choice here, Mrs Pearce. You can stay home and ask your GP to make a house call, you can let us help you walk out to the ambulance or you can wait for us to get assistance to move you.'

'Oh, get lost,' Mrs Pearce snapped. 'I'm not having a bunch of firemen tramping around my house and sniggering because you're not capable of doing your job and carrying me. You're just as bloody useless as anyone else, aren't you?'

'At least she signed the paperwork.'

'Mmm.' Laura was negotiating the rush-hour traffic through the central city. 'Thank goodness we didn't have to transport her.'

'She'll probably call another ambulance in the middle of the night.'

'Won't be our problem.' Laura grinned. 'If she keeps it up she'll go on the blacklist.'

'Doesn't mean we don't have to respond, though.'

'No.' Even people who abused the emergency services to the point that everyone knew them to be time-wasters had to be seen. They couldn't afford to let a genuine incident go unattended. Laura let her breath out in a long sigh. 'It's been quite a day, hasn't it? I'll be glad to get home.'

'You're going home?' Tim sounded surprised. 'Have you decided to let Jase fend for himself, then?'

'No.' Laura felt the heat in her cheeks. 'I meant home to Jason's place.' It hadn't even occurred to her it wasn't 'home'. How could it feel like that when she'd only been in residence for four days?

'Don't let him get too dependent on you, Laura.'

'I won't. This is only temporary. And there's no way he'd manage on his own.'

'Exactly. Don't let him use you.'

'I'm enjoying it,' Laura said sincerely. 'Megan's gorgeous.'

'What about Jason?' Tim seemed to be choosing his words carefully.

'He's gorgeous, too,' Laura said lightly. Then she caught Tim's glance and laughed. 'I was joking, Tim.' Good grief, had somebody other than Mrs McKendry guessed her motivation?

Happily, Tim joined her laughter and her confession was dismissed. 'I meant, is he enjoying it? He was pretty horrified at the prospect of trying out fatherhood.'

'I'm not sure about enjoying it exactly,' Laura admitted. 'But he's getting used to it. He can change a nappy all by himself now and feed her.' She thought about the laughter that had been provoked by teaching Jason how to bathe his daughter last night and smiled. 'Actually, I suspect he is starting to enjoy it—he just doesn't want to.'

'Why not?'

'It's a complication in his life that he wasn't expecting.'

'Has he said anything about the mother?'

'She was a one-night stand.' Laura pulled away as the traffic light changed to green. 'He had trouble remembering her name. What is there to say?'

'I'll bet his girlfriend has had plenty to say about it all.'

'Maxine?' Laura tried to sound offhand. 'She's rung a few times but I'm not sure if Jase has told her why he's so busy.'

'He's not the only one who's too busy. You'll wear yourself out, Laura, if this goes on much longer.'

'The next couple of days will be easier, with Mrs Mack helping.'

'You've still got to take her home after work. It must be like having two full-time jobs.'

It was. Both Laura and Jason were tired at the end of the day shift. It would have been wonderful to sit down and have a beer or two and chill out. Jason was keen to talk about the job they had shared that morning and recapture the thrill of rescuing little Vicky. But little Megan needed feeding and changing and bathing.

Laura did the nappy change by herself. She gave Jason a dirty look when he returned. 'You arranged the timing of that phone call to perfection, didn't you?'

'Not my fault.' Jason smiled winningly. 'Tell you what, I'll do the next two nappy changes.' He tried an effective head tilt and beseeching eyebrow lift. 'Three nappy changes?''

Laura tried not to laugh. 'What do you want, Jase?'

'Well, now you mention it, I kind of told Maxine I might be able to meet her for a quick drink later this evening.'

'But we've got an appointment to take Megan to the GP and have her ears checked.'

'Oh, no! I completely forgot about that.' Jason chewed the inside of his cheek. 'Does she really need to go? She's obviously better, so she doesn't need antibiotics.'

Laura just looked at him. Maybe Megan wasn't in need of a trip to the doctor but, dammit, she wasn't going to babysit while Jason went off to spend time with his girlfriend. She wasn't *that* much of a masochist.

'Oh, damn,' Jason muttered. 'Maxine thinks I'm trying to dump her.'

'Why?'

'Because I keep avoiding her and saying I'm busy.'

'You mean you still haven't told her *why* you're busy?'

'Hell, no. Maxine hates babies. One of the first things she said to me was that I'd better make sure I didn't get her pregnant.'

'Really?' Laura's tone was distinctly waspish. 'Sounds like a wonderful beginning to a meaningful relationship.'

'We don't have a meaningful relationship. We have...'

'Sex?' The word was bitten out and Jason gave her a strange look. Laura tried to lighten up. 'For heaven's sake, Jase. If it's that important to you, I'll take Megan to the doctor by myself. You go out and have sex with Maxine.'

She received an even stranger look. 'We were only planning on a drink, actually.' He turned away. 'Forget it. I'll ring her back and say I can't make it. We'll both take Megan to the doctor.'

'Maybe you should take her and I'll go out with my boyfriend.'

Jason turned back with an astonished expression. 'But you haven't got a boyfriend.'

The easy assumption was galling. 'What makes you so damned sure about that, Jason Halliday?'

He had the grace to look ashamed of himself. 'It's just— I mean... *Have* you got a boyfriend?'

'No, actually. Not at the moment.'

'Well, that's all right, then.' Jason blinked in consternation at the stare he was still receiving and ran his fingers through his hair. 'Isn't it?'

'I suppose it is. In fact, I'm beginning to think that all women might be better off on their own.'

'I didn't mean that.' Jason eyed the door as though planning a hasty exit. 'I meant, it would be all right if you came to the doctor's with me and Megan.'

'Seeing as you've so kindly pointed out that I've got nothing better to do, I may as well.' Laura's tone was wry. 'But don't push it, Jase. I'm not going to look after your daughter while you go out and have a good time with some bimbo.'

The atmosphere was still strained by the time they had returned with a clean bill of health for Megan and a take-away dinner for themselves, which obviated any need to cook. Laura took a shower but found Jason still curiously quiet when she returned in time to give Megan a bedtime bottle at ten p.m.

'Let's hope she sleeps as well as she did last night. It was a bit of a treat only having to get up once, wasn't it?'

'Mmm.' Jason was watching Laura settle herself on the couch with Megan in her arms. She knew her hair was hanging in damp waves like rats' tails and the soft old T-shirt she intended sleeping in clung to her figure quite well enough to reveal how ample her curves were, but did he have to stare at her quite like that? Maybe she'd been less than pleasant about him wanting to go out on a date but she wasn't trying to pass herself off as some kind of saint here. There was no point in getting Jason interested in her by pretending to be something she wasn't. She wasn't *that* desperate.

'Something bothering you, Jase?' Maybe it was time to make a joke out of it all. 'Other than missing out on sex with Maxine, that is?'

Jason scowled. 'Cut it out, Laura. I didn't think you were the bitchy type.'

Laura hung her head, watching Megan suck. Maybe it hadn't come out as lightly as she'd intended because it cut a little too close to the bone. She wasn't the bitchy type, and she'd better start being more careful or Jason would realise why she might be the jealous type. She heard Jason sigh and looked up swiftly.

'You're right, I *was* being bitchy. Sorry. I guess I'm a bit tired...and...'

'And?'

'And I have trouble understanding why you find Maxine so attractive.' If Jason needed a prime example of a bitchy type, he didn't have to look far. Laura had only met Maxine once, when she'd come to meet Jason after work at the station. The frankly dismissive glance she'd received had been enough to know that appearances were all that mattered to Jason's latest conquest.

'She's got great legs.'

'Ah.' Laura managed a smile. 'That makes it all right, then.'

The look they shared acknowledged that Maxine wasn't likely to make the grade long term. They both laughed but Laura's amusement was forced. She *was* tired and she could feel a headache coming on. Adjusting her position to hold the bottle with the hand of the arm holding Megan, Laura removed her glasses with her other hand and gave the bridge of her nose a good rub. She left the glasses on the coffee-table to give her face a rest. Then she kept her gaze on the baby she held as she felt her mouth relax into a soft smile.

Megan was turned a little into her body and one hand was on her breast with its fingers splayed like a tiny starfish. It was pushing and squeezing rhythmically, as though she was being breast-fed and helping the supply along. Laura was astonished at the response it provoked in both her body and heart. She was staring down a bottomless well of emotion from which any amount of love for this infant could be drawn.

And that was disturbing. It hadn't been part of the plan at all. She might end up being more upset by having to hand Megan back to her mother than finding out Jason would never be remotely attracted to her.

The thought prompted a gaze in Jason's direction and Laura caught her breath. He had been watching Megan's hand on her breast as well and his gaze flicked up to catch hers almost guiltily. He stood up, mumbling something about making coffee, but his gaze didn't leave hers until he turned away and that had been quite long enough for Laura to see what she had thought impossible.

Had it simply been wishful thinking?

No. Her own body was on fire right now. She wanted Jason more than she had ever wanted anyone but the flashes of desire she was used to experiencing had been nothing like this. There was a totally new dimension to it now. Only one thing could have caused such an increase in intensity and that was the unmistakable glimpse of sexual awareness she had caught in Jason's gaze.

It wasn't desire exactly, but the knowledge that Jason had woken up to the fact she was a woman was enough.

For now.

CHAPTER SIX

INGLEWOOD station had acquired a new mascot.

By the end of her second day shift, Megan Bates Halliday had earned the nickname of 'Peanut', due to her small size, and had at least half a dozen macho specimens of manhood quite besotted with her. Not that they advertised the fact, of course.

'I'll have a hold, if you have something else you want to do, Jase.'

'Hey, thanks, Cliff. I'm due to do a check on the breathing apparatus filters and valves. Shouldn't take too long.'

'We'll be all right. Take as long as you like.' Cliff adjusted his hold on the baby. 'What do you reckon, Peanut? Shall we see what's on the sports channel?'

When Jason came back, having completed the maintenance duty, he found Megan being held by Stick.

'Wasn't my idea,' Stick said loftily.

'Was so,' Cliff contradicted. 'I suggested a game of snooker to Bruce and you said, "Guess I'll have to have a turn with Peanut, then."'

'You could have left her with Mrs Mack.' Jason noticed that, although Stick was now looking somewhat sheepish, he wasn't in any hurry to offload his burden.

'She's busy washing the floors.'

'Is Laura still out on the road, then?'

'Yeah. They're having a really busy day. I don't think they've even been back for a lunch-break.'

Snooker balls clicked and Cliff whistled appreciatively. '*Nice* shot, Bruce.'

'Six points,' Stick informed Megan. 'Let's put them on the board, shall we?' Megan did appear to be watching as Stick moved the marker to a new score and the cooing noise could easily be read as approval. Stick grinned. 'She's catching on,' he told Jason. 'Pretty smart, isn't she?'

'I like a girl who likes watching snooker.' Cliff was lining up his next shot. 'I reckon she should be the station mascot.'

Stick's nod was enthusiastic. 'I'll bet Mrs Mack could make her a junior-sized uniform. That'd be cute.'

Jason could just imagine Megan as a toddler with a custom-made fireman's jacket and helmet. He could even see her holding his hand as she tottered along beside the life-sized version. Hell, it *would* be cute. He shoved the image aside and held out his arms.

'She's due for a feed,' he said. 'I'm surprised she's not yelling her head off by now.'

'She likes us,' Cliff announced.

'Don't get too attached,' Jason warned. 'I'm not keeping her.'

'Might not be that bad, you know.' Stick's gaze slid away from Jason's raised eyebrows. 'Well, she is kinda cute. For a baby, that is.'

Absurdly, Jason felt proud of the fact that Megan was his daughter as he carried her away from the games room-cum-gymnasium towards the kitchen. She could certainly turn on the charm at times. His colleagues had no idea what she was like when she wasn't happy, though. They wouldn't be anything like as smitten if they had to endure an hour or two of grizzling ill humour.

As he had to that night. There was no pleasure in having a beer while he cooked dinner
listening to that incessant squalling. She quiet-
ened down so that Laura could eat in peace,
he noticed, but he felt obliged to keep walking
round and round the living room in the hope
of getting her off to sleep.

'Did you end up getting any lunch?' he
asked Laura.

'No. This is great, though. What is it?'

'Goulash.'

'Is it?' Laura took another mouthful. 'I can't
taste any paprika.'

'What's paprika?'

'The red stuff that looks like pepper and
goes into goulash.'

'Nah.' Jason skirted the couch and began
another circuit. 'Goulash is just what you make
when you chop up all the leftovers, throw in
some veg and cook it.'

'Whatever. It tastes fantastic.'

Jason eyed his own plate, cooling on the
bench, and sighed. 'So what kept you so
busy?'

'We kicked off with a hypoglycaemic coma,
had a heart attack around nine a.m., a kid fell
off a climbing frame at play centre for morning

tea and then we got stuck with an MVA and entrapment out on the motorway.'

'Who went out to that?' Jason watched carefully to see if he could detect any disappointment on Laura's part that he hadn't arrived. Surely, if she did fancy him, as his mates had suggested, he could pick up a few clues here and there.

'A crew from Central station.' Laura didn't seem at all disappointed.

'They could have called us,' Jason grumbled. 'We spent half the morning putting in smoke alarms for old-age pensioners, had a false alarm at a factory warehouse and then nothing for the rest of the day. It was dead boring.'

'Our afternoon was a bit dull. Non-stop calls but none of them were very exciting. Sore backs, sore hearts, sore legs. You name it, we saw it.'

'How long did the extrication for the MVA take?'

'Two hours.'

'What? We could have done it in less than half the time.'

'So could they, but he wasn't badly injured. We just didn't want to do anything that might exacerbate his neck injury so we put on a neck brace and gave him oxygen and basically kept him amused while the fire boys cut up the car all around him.'

'Still shouldn't have taken two hours. What was it, an armoured truck?'

Laura laughed. 'No, it was a Mini and he was a very large man. We ended up taking off the roof and lifting him out with a crane.'

'That would have been embarrassing. Especially on the motorway.'

'Quite a few people stopped to have a look,' Laura said. 'Maybe the embarrassment will motivate him to lose a bit of weight.' She picked up another forkful of her meal and looked at it thoughtfully. 'I'm a great one to talk, aren't I? And here I am, stuffing myself.'

'You're not fat,' Jason assured her.

'I'm not exactly skinny either.'

'Women who are naturally skinny are few and far between. The ones who are obsessed with being unnaturally skinny usually have a hell of a lot of other hang-ups as well. Believe me,' Jason said firmly. 'I'm speaking from experience here.'

'So why do you always pick skinny girlfriends, then?'

'Dunno.' Jason tried to sound offhand. 'Maybe I'll go for curvy next time.'

Megan's fractious cry distracted him from trying to assess whether Laura had responded to that fishing expedition. The quiet period was definitely over.

'Maybe she's got another ear infection.'

'I think she's just overtired,' Laura said. 'Maybe she should have been sleeping on station today, instead of being used for some pass-the-parcel game. Has it turned into some sort of competition to see who can spend the most time playing with the baby or something?'

'If you ask me, we're lucky that the guys are happy to have her around at all.'

'It's a night shift tomorrow. They won't be so happy if their sleep gets interrupted.' Laura stopped eating, her fork poised. 'What will we do if we're both called out at the same time?'

'Mackie's offered to sleep on station for two nights.' Jason sighed heavily as Megan paused only long enough to take in a deep enough breath to raise her volume. 'I've had about enough of this,' he muttered. 'It's been a week, Peanut. Where the hell is your mother?'

'Here, I'll take her.' Laura dropped her fork and her chair scraped as she pushed it back hurriedly. 'That was really nice, thanks. You'd better have yours before it's too cold.'

It was already too cold. Jason grimaced around his mouthful and eyed the microwave as he chewed, but he was too hungry to be bothered reheating his meal and the second mouthful didn't taste so bad.

Megan grizzled on intermittently. Laura looked fed up but Jason stubbornly took his time to eat. Perversely, he welcomed the increase in tension because it made him forget any disturbing thoughts that Laura might be helping him because she wanted more than friendship from him. It also effectively blotted out any of the brief fantasies he'd been experiencing about still having the kid around when she was old enough to hold his hand and walk beside him. Or go off to school with a cute little backpack. Or smile when her front baby teeth had been purchased by the tooth fairy.

He didn't offer to relieve Laura when he'd finished eating either. She couldn't complain about him clearing the bench, could she? He knew he was pushing his luck when he popped the tab on a can of beer and turned the television set on, but what was the worst thing that could happen here? Laura would go home, he'd be left with a baby he couldn't possibly manage on his own and he'd have to stop procrastinating and do something about finding Shelley Bates.

The scenario was unlikely, in any case. Laura seemed quite happy to do more than her share most of the time, and why not? She was female, wasn't she? Didn't they all get a bit clucky by the time they were pushing thirty? He was doing her a favour, really, by showing what that genetic programming could land you with.

Within a few minutes, however, it became apparent that a surprising hiccup could be occurring in Laura Green's genetic programming.

'What do you think you're doing, Jase?'

'Sorry. Did you want a beer?'

'No.'

'Come and watch this programme, then. This forensic pathologist is great at solving murder mysteries.'

'There'll be a murder around here soon and it won't be at all mysterious.'

Jason grinned. 'I know how you feel. She's a bit of a pain when she won't go to sleep, isn't she?'

'Right.' Laura's lips compressed into a grim line. 'That's *it*. I've had enough.'

Megan landed on Jason's lap with enough speed to provoke an outraged wail. While a reprimand was undeniably justified, Jason was alarmed to see Laura heading for the back door of the house.

'Where are you going?''

'Out.'

'When will you be back?' Jason was sorry he'd taken her assistance for granted now. Really sorry. The faint note of panic in his tone was quite genuine and he could feel himself go a shade paler when the only response he received from Laura was the slamming of the back door.

He'd done it now. He was up the creek without a paddle and he knew quite well he deserved it. Laura had turned her life upside down for the last week in order to help him and she'd done it with remarkably good humour and competence. She'd had a much busier day than he'd had today and yet he'd been enough of a bastard to expect her to keep going. Jason groaned. If he'd wanted to find a way of ensuring Laura didn't want him for a friend, let alone anything more, he'd found it without any effort at all.

He'd just have to make up for it somehow. Find something nice to do that would let Laura know how much he appreciated her. But what? Jason's idea of looking after a woman generally involved some quality physical contact, and that wasn't an option with Laura.

Or was it?

Unbidden, the image of seeing Laura feeding Megan last night surfaced. The full, soft-looking outline of her breast had been made startlingly obvious by the movements of that tiny hand. Jason had never seen Laura without her spectacles on before either, and when she'd looked up at him he had been struck by eyes that had reminded him of melted chocolate. Recognising that Laura was actually a rather attractive woman had been a shock. Like that time his kid sister had brought her first boy-friend home.

But him and Laura? No way. She was so far removed from what he considered to be his type it was inconceivable. Not that she wouldn't make someone a fantastic wife and mother, but it was precisely those qualities that put her into a friendship rather than relation-ship category. She was fun to have around. They could have a laugh, the way they did at work. Laura was one of the boys. Hell, she even liked beer! And when life wasn't so much fun Laura was prepared to help and he knew by now that he could trust her not to jump ship when the going got tough.

At least, he had up until he'd pushed her to breaking point. He didn't deserve a mate like Laura and he wouldn't have her around much longer unless he found some way to apologise. Trying to come up with an idea was enough of a challenge to distract Jason throughout an entire nappy change so that it was no more than a vaguely unpleasant duty.

'I've got it!' he told Megan as he pushed her feet into the leg holes of a clean stretchsuit. 'Mummy's tired. And what do women like to do most when they're tired?'

He needed three goes on some of those pesky, undersized stud buttons. 'I've seen the ads,' he explained. 'They like a soak in a hot bath, with candles and nice smelly stuff and a glass of wine.'

The plan was excellent. Brilliant, even if he did say so himself, but it was a little harder to execute than he'd anticipated. The triumph of finding a single, well-used decorative candle in the depths of a kitchen cupboard was dimmed by the unavailability of any perfume or bubble bath.

'A bit of dishwashing liquid would make some bubbles, wouldn't it?' He conferred with the baby he was carrying on one arm. 'But what smells nice?'

Another one-handed fossick in the cupboards began, and Megan started to feel heavy. Jason briefly considered trying out that front pack contraption Laura had persuaded him to purchase on that expensive visit to Baby Warehouse but he dismissed the thought. There was something disturbingly permanent about attaching a baby to your body like that. Holding her tucked casually into the crook of one arm was a kind of insurance policy. She could be put down or passed on to someone else with no effort required at all. The way she was handed around at the station was becoming part of the routine. One of the guys was always hovering somewhere nearby, waiting for a turn and pretending not to be. Wouldn't work at all if they had to deal with buckles and straps, and it would look ridiculous. Who wanted to look like a kangaroo with a pouch in dire need of mending?

At least this search was satisfyingly brief.

'There you go,' he told his daughter. 'Perseverance pays off, kid. Cinnamon. And vanilla. They both smell nice.' He eyed the tin of formula on the kitchen bench but Megan seemed happy enough for the moment to be ferried back and forth by a man on a mission.

'Dammit,' Jason exclaimed a short time later. 'We've got a wineglass but no wine. Do you think juice might do instead?' Changing arms to ease the ache of tired muscles, Jason's eye caught the tin of formula again. 'I'd better feed you in a minute, Peanut, hadn't I?' Big, blue eyes stared up at him. 'Laura won't enjoy her soak if she has to listen to you whingeing because I haven't fed you.'

Megan wasn't whingeing right now. She appeared to be listening intently to the deep, soft voice that had become much more familiar over the last hour. Her gaze was still fastened on Jason's and he braced himself as her face crinkled and her lips moved. But no cry emerged from that rosebud mouth. The facial contortion continued and suddenly, totally un-expectedly, Jason found that the tiny person he was holding was smiling at him.

It was Megan's first smile and it was for *him*.

She *liked* him.

A warm glow started somewhere deep within Jason and then grew and grew until it felt like something was about to burst. It was unlike anything he'd ever felt in his life.

Dammit! Why wasn't Laura here to see this? Megan was *smiling*. The corners of her lips curled up even more and her lips parted to make her look as though she was silently and joyously laughing. Jason felt so ridiculously pleased and proud that he didn't give a damn that his eyes were prickling. He wanted to cry. Or laugh. Or shout out the news. Instead, he did something that seemed far more appropriate.

He smiled back.

Laura walked swiftly, pushing herself despite the physical weariness that made her bones feel like lead. Her spiritual weariness was far more of a concern. This was never going to work. OK, she'd established a friendship with

Jason. She'd seen evidence that he could find her attractive. She might even succeed in winning herself a place in his life, but where would that leave her? Precisely where she would have ended up with John, that's where. Making all the effort and putting up with all the crap because *she* wanted the relationship to work so much more than he did.

Jason might only be having a beer and watching television because he felt like it now, but it would only be a matter of time before he was off to the pub with his mates or having an affair, like John, because that took his fancy, and if Laura wanted to keep him around she'd just have to deal with it.

Escaping the empty shell that her relationship with John had become had led to a vow that she would never again become involved with anyone who didn't love her as much as she loved them. Yet here she was, trying to set herself up with an even more heartbreaking arrangement. Jason wouldn't just expect his dinner on the table or a bit of company on the odd night he chose to stay at home. He'd want his child raised as well. A child who was rapidly claiming a large portion of the love Laura was only too ready to bestow.

Why can't love be more equally distributed? Laura directed the silent question to the post-box at the end of Crighton Terrace as she finally neared the end of her long walk. She picked up her pace a little until she got past the empty and semi-derelict two-storied house on the corner. All that Laura wanted was to receive the same kind of love she was so capable of giving. Was that too much to ask?

Too much to ask of Jason Halliday, she decided bitterly as she opened the back door of his house. His idea of love was probably giving a girl a good time in bed. He didn't have a committed bone in his body when it came to women, and he probably didn't need to. With his looks and personality he wouldn't face any problem finding someone prepared to do the running to make things work when he finally decided to settle down.

But it wouldn't be her. No way. She wouldn't marry Jason if he—

Her passage into the living room was abruptly halted by what she saw in front of her. Jason lay flat on his back on the couch. One arm and one leg were draped over the side and an almost empty baby's bottle rested on the floor close to the dangling hand. He was deeply asleep, his lips slightly parted, his hair tousled and his features softened enough to make him look years younger. Vulnerable, almost.

Megan lay sprawled on top of her father, stomach to stomach, and she was also soundly asleep. There was no danger of her rolling off, though. Jason's arm was almost completely encircling the infant and he had his thumb safely anchored in a belt loop of his jeans.

Laura sighed softly, overwhelmed by the wave of pure love the scene evoked in her. Any good intentions she had to extricate herself from giving more than she could ever hope to receive flew out the window. There was no way she could walk away from either of them. Not when she felt like this. Whatever happened, she was going to see this through as far as it went.

Quietly, Laura moved further into the room, planning to bypass the couch and head for the bathroom for a much-needed shower. But Jason's eyelids flickered open.

'Hey...you came back!'

'Yeah.' Laura spoke as softly as he had. 'I'm a masochist.'

'Guess what?'

'What?'

'Megan smiled at me.'

'Really?' Laura saw the delight in Jason's sleepy grin and that wash of emotion she had experienced on entering the room returned with renewed strength. 'That's so cool! I wish I'd seen it.'

'You *should* have been here,' Jason admonished. Then he seemed to wake up enough to remember why she hadn't been there, and his expression held a mixture of apology and relief. 'At least you're back now.'

'Mmm.' Laura didn't want to spoil the moment by discussing her walkout. 'I need a shower. Are you OK with Megan for a bit longer?'

'Take as long as you like.' Jason closed his eyes and smiled. 'Enjoy,' he added rather smugly.

Laura had taken the tone to be self-congratulatory because he was minding the baby, but she changed her mind as she stepped into the bathroom and closed the door behind her.

The bath was full, almost to the brim, and sparse blobs of bubbles like small clouds floated amongst faint tendrils of steam. It smelt vaguely like some sort of pudding her mother used to make and her awareness of the scent was heightened by the dim, flickering light emanating from the depths of a hollow, orange candle. Beside the candle was something that was her final undoing. A stemmed wineglass, filled with what looked suspiciously like beer.

It was no reason to cry. This was a present—an opportunity to relax and indulge herself—and here she was, standing on the tiled floor with tears streaming down her face. Laura scrubbed the tears away with her hand and managed a wobbly smile as she pulled off her clothes. Jason had done this for her, and he must have used virtually the whole time she'd been out to do it because it looked like he'd cleaned the bathroom before creating her treat. He must have been thinking about her the whole time, possibly coping simultaneously with a grizzly baby, and he had harnessed clearly limited resources to produce something that was purely for her benefit.

John would never have done something like this for her, not in a million years. Jason cared. He *really* cared, and that was far more meaningful than any sexual awareness she might be able to stir in him. Laura climbed into the tub and lay back, resting her head on the rim and allowing a few more tears to wash away the despair she had carried with her on her solitary walk. She had been wrong. It *could* work out between her and Jason. And even if it didn't, she would never forget this bath for as long as she lived.

The call to an unconscious woman on the next night duty became the first strong reminder when Laura and Tim were led by a panicked husband into the bathroom of the patient's house.

'It's my wife, Irene,' he was explaining as he rushed ahead of them down a narrow hallway. 'She was just having a soak in the bath and then I heard this almighty crash and came in to find her lying on the floor with blood everywhere. I thought she was *dead*!'

Irene Spelling wasn't dead but she wasn't feeling at all well. She was also highly embarrassed by the ineffective covering a towel was affording.

'Do you know what happened?' Laura asked.

'I came over all funny when I stood up. Next thing I know I'm lying on the floor and my head hurts.'

A superficial scalp wound caused by grazing her head on the corner of the vanity unit had produced copious amounts of blood, but the facecloth Irene was pressing to the area had it under control for the moment. Laura was more concerned by potential causes for the faint.

'How are you feeling now, Irene?'

'Like I'm going to be sick. And there's a funny ringing noise in my ears.'

'Let's lie you down,' Laura directed. 'And lift your legs a bit.' Irene's husband assisted by sitting on the toilet seat and holding her feet on his lap. 'Can you get a blood pressure, please, Tim?'

Tim was fitting an oxygen mask on Irene's face. He reached for the blood-pressure cuff as Laura started peeling the backs off the electrodes needed to get more information about what was happening in Irene's cardiovascular system.

The bath had been a hot one—Laura could feel the steamy heat surrounding them. Just as well it didn't smell like a pudding, Laura thought fleetingly, or she might have trouble concentrating on what she was supposed to be doing.

The heat of the water and surrounding air could have caused a level of vasodilation enough to interfere with the normal mechanisms that adjusted blood pressure to posture. The reduction in blood supply to the heart had a knock-on effect of reducing supply to the brain, and was a common enough cause for fainting, but Laura needed to rule out any more serious cause such an underlying cardiac condition or reaction to medications.

'Your ECG looks fine,' she reassured Irene and her husband a minute later. 'You don't have any heart problems that you know of, do you?'

'No.'

'Anything else you're being treated for?'

'No. Well...' Irene looked embarrassed again. 'I'm taking some of that new stuff that's supposed to help you lose weight.'

'BP's 100 over 50,' Tim reported.

'That's a bit on the low side,' Laura explained. 'But it's only to be expected if you've had a fainting episode. Do you know what your blood pressure normally is?'

'I think it's a bit high. My doctor told me it was another reason I needed to lose weight. I am trying. I've hardly eaten anything today, have I, Colin?'

'No,' her husband confirmed. 'Just rabbit food.'

'That might have been a contributing factor to the faint,' Laura said. 'We'll check your blood sugar and then I'll have a look at where you hit your head.' Irene had 'come over all funny' well before she'd come into contact with the vanity unit and she appeared quite alert now so a head injury was unlikely to have been responsible for the period of unconsciousness, but Laura intended to make a thorough check.

Fifteen minutes later, both she and Tim were satisfied that Irene was fine.

'I'm feeling ever so much better,' she informed them.

'BP's up to 130 over 90,' Tim reported.

'Blood sugar's normal.' Laura dropped the small finger-pricking device into the sharps container. 'And everything else checks out. There's really no need for us to take you into hospital, Irene, but if you or Colin need any more reassurance then we're happy to do so.'

'No, I'm fine,' Irene insisted. 'All I want to do is get dressed and have some supper.'

'Good idea.' Tim smiled. 'We're about due for some supper ourselves.'

'Would you like a cup of tea before you go?' Irene pushed her arms into the dressing-gown Laura was holding for her. 'I've got a lovely banana cake that my daughter brought round this afternoon.'

'That's very kind of you but we'll have to get back on station,' Laura said with a smile.

Tim caught Laura's eye as she coiled the lead wires and slotted them back into a pocket of the life pack. 'With a bit of luck there might even be a muffin left for us.'

'Oh, take the cake with you,' Irene exclaimed. 'I shouldn't be eating it anyway and Colin hates banana cake.'

'No, you deserve a treat after this,' Laura said. 'You enjoy it.'

'But I'll only eat one piece and the rest will be wasted. I'd really like you to take it.'

'Please, do,' Colin added. 'By way of thanks. We're very grateful for your help. I

was scared stiff. I had no idea of what to do
other than call for an ambulance.'

'We're happy to help. We shouldn't accept
cake.'

'Wow—cake! You shouldn't have!'

Jason, Stick, Cliff and Bruce eyed the offering that Laura carried into the commonroom.

'Hey—you've already eaten some.'

They had left a segment with Irene by way
of a compromise. The rest of the banana cake
was clearly going to be appreciated immedi-
ately by everyone on Green Watch at
Inglewood station. Or it would have been, if
not for the arrival of an unexpected visitor.

'Maxine!' Jason put down the plate he was
holding and stepped out of the cake queue.
'What are you doing here?'

'Came to see you, of course.' The willowy
redhead sounded less than happy. 'I want to
know why you're avoiding me, Jason
Halliday.'

'I'm not.' Jason's smile was one of his most
winning and Laura's heart fell. He'd smooth
over the troubled waters and she could just see

herself babysitting Megan while he went out to make things up with Maxine.

'Here.' Stick could see the banana cake disappearing with alarming rapidity. 'You take Peanut.' He shoved the bundle he held into Jason's arms. 'She's your kid after all.'

Laura could swear that Stick flashed her the ghost of a wink. He must have known what effect his action and words would have. Laura gained a rather savage sense of satisfaction from the expression on Maxine's face, but Stick didn't seem to have finished stirring troubled waters. He grinned as Megan produced noisy evidence of the biological functions occurring in her small body.

'Hey, Jase. She's inherited your talent for burping and farting at the same time.'

The rest of Green Watch found Stick's observation hilarious.

'There goes the court case,' Bruce commiserated. 'That's even more of a genetic link than the colour of her eyes, mate.'

Jason looked as though he was desperately hoping the ground would open beneath his feet. Megan was looking a lot happier than she had a moment ago and was beaming approval at her father.

'Um…Jason?'

'Yeah?' Jason's smile looked glued on now but he was still bravely standing his ground.

'Do you want to tell me what's going on?'

The rest of Green Watch now seemed totally absorbed in their supper. 'Great cake,' Bruce announced. 'Isn't it, Stick?'

'The best.' Stick nodded. He glanced sideways at Jason and then caught Cliff's eye and winked.

'Jason?'

Stick wasn't being quite as successful as the others in hiding his interest in the building confrontation but Laura projected what she hoped was a calm indifference.

'I think I'll have some cake, too,' Laura murmured. 'It does look nice.'

'You need it,' Stick told her a little too loudly. 'You're fading away, Laura. Being a mum is taking it out of you.'

'I wish.' Laura grinned. She could appreciate the efforts of these guys as they closed a protective rank around her and tried to let her know that they considered her to be just as good as the gorgeous redhead now taking centre stage in the commonroom. But Stick did have a point. Her clothes were definitely feeling a lot looser than they had a week or two ago. Her pleasure in someone else noticing was heightened by the glare she could feel coming from Maxine.

'So, you've been ''busy'', have you, Jason?' Maxine used long, French-manicured nails to make the quotation marks in the air. 'I'd say you were pretty busy nine months ago or so as well.' She narrowed her eyes at Laura. 'With *her*?'

'No, of course not,' Jason assured her. Then he blinked. What was so 'of course' about it, anyway?

Lightning-fast thoughts flashed through his brain. Yes, Laura wore glasses but now that he had noticed the colour of her eyes they seemed more like frames that accentuated rather than hid them. Yes, she was short and Jason had always avoided short women because they made him feel like a father figure, but Laura was anything but childish. She could be bossy but she was never bad-tempered without a jolly good reason and, what's more, she was bloody good at her job. Yes, she was nothing like as skinny as Maxine, but he'd actually been serious when he'd told Laura he might try some curves next time. And on top of everything else, he simply liked Laura. Right now, it seemed that she had more going for her than Maxine did.

'Laura's a friend,' he explained. 'A very good friend. And she's living with me right now to help look after Megan.'

'Megan?'

'My daughter.' There was an unmistakable note of pride in Jason's voice and his colleagues exchanged meaningful glances over their slices of cake. 'Here, would you like to hold her?'

'Not in this lifetime,' Maxine said sweetly. 'Why didn't you tell me you had a baby, Jason?'

'But I didn't have a baby,' Jason said. 'Not until last week.'

'I've spoken to you since last week.' Maxine looked confused but then licked her lips and shook her tumble of tresses into place. 'You still could have told me.'

'I thought I would have got rid of it by now.'

'Oh.' Maxine looked a little happier. 'You're not keeping it, then?'

'No. Its mother's coming back. *Her* mother,' Jason amended. He didn't like the way talking to Maxine was sucking him back in time. Had

he really thought her such an amazing conquest? She hadn't even *looked* at Megan, let
alone said how cute she was. How self-centred
could someone get? 'At least, we think she is.'

'You don't know?'

'No.' Jason was suddenly rather pleased to
be holding Megan in his arms. 'It's possible
she's never coming back,' he found himself
saying. 'So I might end up being pretty busy
for the next ten years or so. Are you sure you
don't want to hold her, Maxine? Look, she's
smiling.'

Maxine's look said it all. Everybody studi-
ously stuffed themselves with cake for the next
few minutes as Jason's relationship went
through some speedy death throes. Laura
found her throat too constricted to swallow,
however. Jason had just been made very firmly
single again, and Jason never stayed single for
long. Just how far from home would he go
looking for a replacement for the beautiful
Maxine? Maybe he wouldn't bother looking at
all for a while. He might even be upset by the
break-up. She watched anxiously from the corner of her eye as he turned back from the doorway where his final words and probably an
apology to Maxine had gone unheeded.

'Hey, have you lot eaten all that cake?' Jason shook his head sadly. 'Oink, oink!'

'You can have mine,' Laura offered. Relief that Jason wasn't noticeably devastated at the break-up of yet another relationship made her smile widely. 'I've only eaten half.'

'Thanks, Laura.' Jason sat down beside her and swapped the baby for the cake plate. 'I knew I could count on you.'

Laura smiled at Megan. Jason focussed on the half-slice of banana cake and neither of them was aware of the new wave of meaningful glances exchanged in the room.

Or the rather satisfied-looking smiles.

CHAPTER SEVEN

'DID you have anything specific in mind?'

Laura stared at her reflection in the huge mirror facing her. Her peripheral vision took in the figure of the young hairdresser who was also eyeing the thick, mousy, one-length hair she had just combed out.

'Just a trim, I guess.' Laura's nose wrinkled as she continued to stare at herself. 'It's been at least a year since it had a good cut and the ends must be horribly split.'

'How do you normally wear it?' The length of her hair was now wound around the hairdresser's hand and was being scooped up to sit in a heap on top of her head. She caught her client's gaze in the mirror and Laura grinned.

'Not like that,' she said. 'I just tie it back in a ponytail to keep it out of the way.'

The hair was released and then fluffed out by expert fingers. 'You've got quite a bit of natural curl, you know. It's just too heavy in one length for it to show. Have you ever thought of having it layered?'

'But then I wouldn't be able to tie it back. I'm a paramedic. I can't have my hair flopping into a patient's face when I'm leaning over them.'

'So why not cut it a bit shorter? You could still have it down to your shoulders if you want to keep the length. If it's layered and shaped it would sit neatly around your face. Look.' The hair got gathered up and pulled back firmly as it would be in a ponytail. 'Like this, all you see is your face.'

'And my glasses.' Laura grimaced. 'I've never noticed how much like a car's head-lamps they look.'

The hold on her hair loosened and changed so that thick loops hung forward, covering the sides of her spectacles and framing her fore-head. Amazingly, the glasses became far less noticeable and the whole appearance of Laura's face softened.

'Hmm. I rather like that.'

The hairdresser was still playing with her tresses. 'What about the colour?'

Laura sighed. 'Dead mouse, I'd call it.'

Her stylist grinned. 'It's not that bad. You've got a lot of blonde in there. A few highlights would bring it out. How much time have you got this morning?'

'As long as I like.' Laura's sigh was much happier this time. Jason had insisted she have the morning to herself to do whatever she felt like doing. Right now, she felt like making a real effort to improve her appearance. 'I'm sold,' she told the hairdresser. 'Go for it. Do whatever you like.'

'Cool. Let's get stuck into the highlights first, then. Shouldn't take more than an hour and a half.'

Ninety minutes of sheer self-indulgence. Bliss. Laura browsed through magazines but couldn't find an article that was more interesting than what was already going on in her head.

That magic wand that had apparently been waved over Inglewood station the morning Megan had arrived seemed to have been used for another small swish in the last couple of days—Laura suspected it had happened during Maxine's visit to the station—and another fundamental change was occurring in her world.

It hadn't happened quite yet but the building anticipation was undeniable and rather delicious. Yesterday had been a little shaky, admittedly. It had been their first day off after a night shift, and she and Jason had taken turns catching up on some sleep, but Jason emerged from his afternoon nap with a very uncharacteristically subdued manner.

'You OK?' Laura had queried. 'You can get some more sleep if you want. Megan's happy.'

'Nah. If I do that I won't sleep tonight and then I'll still be tired tomorrow.'

'Do you want to go out tonight? I'll baby-sit.'

'Who with?' Jason had sounded resigned rather than heartbroken.

'Stick,' Laura had suggested promptly. 'Or Mitch. You haven't had a night out with your mates for ages.'

'They're not my mates any more,' Jason had said darkly. 'How am I supposed to keep the rent up on this place by myself?' His face had brightened momentarily. 'Hey, you don't want to move in, do you Laura? Even if Megan goes home, you'd make a great flatmate.'

If Megan went home? Maybe the comment to Maxine hadn't just been an escape route for the moment. The thought of being a 'flatmate' for Jason was less than appealing, however.

'Sorry, Jase. I already own a house. My best friend, Charlie, is living with me at the moment to help pay the mortgage. Anyway, I'm sure Stick and Mitch will come back once things are back to normal.'

'They prefer Cliff's sleepout,' Jason reminded her. 'It's cheaper. You must have heard them going on about their plans to save up and buy a house together. They're going to live in it and do it up on their days off and then sell it for a huge profit and start again.'

Jason's heavy sigh reminded Laura of more than just any conversations that had been ongoing at work. His mood was understandable. In fact, it was remarkable that he hadn't been plunged into the depths of depression, really. Maxine's exit from his life had probably underscored just how much had changed in a very short period of time. Jason had become a father, had had a bomb detonated under his lifestyle both at work and especially at home; his mates had not only defected from living with him, they were now planning an exciting project that he was excluded from; and his girlfriend had dumped him. He had a lot to think about.

As did Laura.

Jason had not only made more than one reference to the possibility that Shelley might not be riding in on a white charger to rescue him from the parental predicament he found himself in, he'd actually hinted that he wouldn't be overly pleased if she *did*.

Laura had tentatively tested the waters last night by voicing the suggestion that it might be time to try tracking Megan's mother down. Surprisingly, Jason had vetoed the idea with an almost disgusted shake of his head.

'She knows where her baby is,' he'd muttered. 'And if she gave a damn she would have at least made contact by now to see if she's OK.' The clearing of his throat made it seem as though Jason had made a decision. 'I reckon Megan's better off where she is.'

'She won't be able to stay in the country very long on a visitor's permit,' Laura pointed out. 'It's only a matter of months, isn't it? And she won't be able to leave the country without explaining what she's done with her baby.'

'We'll deal with that when it happens,' Jason decreed. 'If that's OK with you, Laura.'

It was more than OK. They were a team and they were both fighting in Megan's corner.

*   *   *

Laura's new hairstyle was also more than OK. Laura was delighted when she walked out of the salon. She was even more delighted when she saw Jason's expression.

'Nice' was the only word of approbation but his eyes were saying a great deal more and Laura tucked her impressions away with all the other things that seemed to be coated with fairy dust.

'Your turn now,' Laura told Jason. 'You get to have the afternoon off to do whatever you like.'

'How 'bout a drive somewhere? We could take Megan to the beach. I'll bet she's never seen a beach.'

'I haven't seen one myself for a while.' Laura also tucked away the fact that Jason had given up an afternoon's reprieve in order to spend time with her and Megan.

As usual they took Laura's hatchback car, because Jason still hadn't cleaned out his own vehicle and she had declared it a health hazard for babies the first time they had taken Megan home. She wasn't about to suggest he spend his free afternoon catching up with that task, though, not when the prospect of a family-type outing was in the offing for the first time.

And it was great.

They drove out of the city, taking the coastal road to the wide expanses of Paraparaumu beach. The warm spring afternoon held all the promise of a hot summer to come, and while the water was still far too cold to contemplate even a paddle, Jason eyed the gentle surf longingly.

'Do you remember summer holidays when you were a kid?'

'My family had a bach at Waihi. Corrugated iron walls, outside loo, no electricity. Must have been hell for Mum but we loved it. We'd spend the whole of January there some years.'

'Good surf?'

Laura laughed. 'Don't tell me you really *are* an ex-surfer?'

'What does she mean?' Jason directed the question to the baby he was holding as they walked along the firm, damp sand just out of reach of the waves. 'Look, Peanut.' He turned his daughter and held her face outwards to the view. 'This is a New Zealand beach,' he said proudly. 'It's where most of us live for the summer holidays. We swim and build sand-castles and have picnics and barbecues. And *surf*,' he added firmly. 'There's nothing better than catching a wave, kid. When you're big enough I'll get you a boogie board and teach you how to use it.'

Except that Megan would probably be spending her Januarys in a cold, grey city on the other side of the world, but neither of them mentioned that.

They sat for a while amongst the tussock-covered sand dunes and Jason was the one who fed Megan. He laughed at the baby's expression on tasting her milk.

'Yeah, I know it's cold. Food always tastes different at the beach. Better,' he added wistfully. He glanced up at Laura. 'Look at that—she's not bothered that it's cold. She's a little trouper, isn't she?'

'She's great,' Laura said quietly.

Jason broke the short silence that fell a minute or two later. 'Talking about food at the beach…I'm *starving*.'

'I'm not surprised. It's three o'clock and we haven't had lunch. Did you see that fish-and-chip shop we passed just down the road?'

'Let's go.' Jason put Megan upright against his shoulder and was rubbing her back with what seemed like an automatic gesture. She obliged by burping loudly only seconds later, and then Jason was on his feet. 'She's going to need a nap soon.'

'She'll sleep in the car.'

'We could take a longer route home. I'll drive this time, if you like. Let's go over the hills and back through the Hutt Valley. I haven't been out that way for years.'

Neither had Laura. 'I never knew there was an animal park out here. Look, it says it has deer and donkeys and goats and you're allowed to feed them all. Be great fun for kids.'

'We'll bring Megan some time when she's awake.'

'She might be a bit young to appreciate it.'

'We're not, though.' Jason turned to grin at Laura but she clutched at his arm.

'Look out, Jase!'

Jason swore roundly as a car, passing them at speed on the downhill stretch, cut in way too sharply. 'What's he in such a big hurry for? Idiot.'

The black BMW containing the idiot had reached the bottom of the slope. Laura's mouth gaped as she saw the swerve when its outside wheels left the tarmac. An instant later, the car had vanished.

'Oh, my God—it's gone over the bank!'

Jason already had the hazard lights on Laura's car flashing. He pulled off the road well before the bend so that oncoming traffic would see the vehicle.

'Stay here,' he ordered. 'I'll go and see what's happened.'

'We know what's happened. That was a hell of a crash we just heard. It's highly likely that someone's injured. I'm coming, too.'

'But we can't just leave Megan.'

'She's sound asleep and perfectly safe in her car seat.' Laura was pulling her first-aid kit, in a small green backpack, from the back of her car. 'Come on, Jason. We're wasting time.'

The bank was steep. They could see the wheels of the unfortunate car, one still spinning, as it lay upside down towards the bottom of the bank. They couldn't see any occupants due to the shrubby undergrowth beneath the trees. Laura's foot slipped as she scrambled down after Jason and he caught her arm and steadied her.

'Careful, babe,' he warned. 'Take it slowly.' He released her arm but took hold of her hand instead and Laura was quite happy to make the journey a team effort. He was quite right, of course. The first rule for any rescuer was not to become one of the casualties, and it would be only too easy to slip and break an ankle or wrist on terrain like this when she was wearing trainers rather than her heavy work boots.

Jason was equally careful as they neared the wreck. 'Don't go downhill from the vehicle,' he warned. 'It's not secure enough to be safe. Can you smell any fuel?'

'No.' Laura sniffed again just to be sure.

'Good. Neither do I.' Jason peered into one of the back windows of the vehicle. 'I can't see anyone.'

Laura looked at where the driver's window was half-buried in soft earth. Or had the roof been compressed that far down? She knelt down and found she could see more than she expected of the front seats. Unexpectedly, she couldn't see any people. Had Jason missed seeing someone crumpled behind the front seats on the roof that was now the floor of the vehicle perhaps?

'Hello!' She called. 'Can anyone hear me?'

'There's a branch been knocked off this tree.' Jason picked up what could have passed for a tree trunk with ease. 'I'll see if I can jam it somewhere on the other side to stabilise the— What the…!' Jason dropped the tree branch and spun around. His laugh was one of embarrassed relief. 'It's a *dog*!' he exclaimed. 'I thought someone was grabbing my leg.'

The dog was black and curly and very fat. It cringed at the first movement from Jason but then wiggled apologetically closer and sat on his foot.

'It's shaking,' Laura observed. 'It's probably been thrown clear of the car.'

'Doesn't look like it's hurt too badly.' Jason moved his foot but the dog moved swiftly and recaptured the contact. 'It's OK,' Jason told it. 'You're safe now. Can you get out of the way so we can find your owner?'

Jason was satisfied enough with his positioning of the branch to let them confirm that the car was empty. The dog obviously hadn't been the only passenger to be thrown clear of the wreck. They searched the surrounding area in expanding circles, with Jason still insisting that Laura take the higher ground.

'Up here!' Laura shouted a minute later. 'I've found someone.'

'He can't have been wearing a seat belt, then.' Jason was beside her within seconds. 'How is he?'

'Unconscious but breathing well,' Laura told him. 'I can't see any major head injury. We'll have to assume he was the only one in the car for the moment. Can you come behind his head and keep his neck stable?'

'Sure. Do you think he's got a spinal injury?'

'Given the mechanism of injury, it's fairly high on the index of suspicion.' Laura checked her phone but the reception had been patchy enough on the road when she had first alerted the emergency services. It had gone completely now and she would not be able to give them an update on the situation. Turning back to the accident victim, Laura ran her hands over the middle-aged man in a body sweep for any obvious bleeding. 'He's got a fractured femur,' she told Jason, pointing to the obvious misalignment of the man's leg. She carried on with a rapid secondary survey. 'Pelvis is stable, that's good.' She was ripping open a woollen bush shirt as they heard a call from above.

'Do you need any help?'

'Have you got a phone?'

'Yes.'

'Call triple one,' Laura directed. 'Tell them we have one patient. No entrapment. Ask them how long it will be before they get here.'

'And check on our baby, would you?' Jason yelled. 'She's in the back seat of our car.'

Our baby. Our car. But Laura couldn't afford to take the time to savour the feeling the words gave her. Her patient was regaining consciousness and groaning loudly.

'Don't try to move,' Laura said. 'It's all right. You've been in an accident but you're safe now.'

The reassurance in Laura's tone was enough to attract the fat black dog, which lay down on its stomach and then wriggled forward like a snake until its nose was right beside Jason's hand.

'Hello again,' Jason said. 'You all right, dog?'

A long, curly black tail wagged in an embarrassed fashion.

The groans from the dog's owner were becoming intelligible words. Laura hung her stethoscope around her neck, satisfied that her patient did not have a chest injury severe enough to interfere with his breathing.

'Keep still,' she said again. 'You may have hurt your neck or back.'

'I...I'm fine,' the man groaned. 'Let me sit up.'

'Not yet.' Laura kept a restraining hand on the man's shoulder. 'What's your name?'

'Bill Treffers. What's yours?'

'I'm Laura. I'm a paramedic. And that's Jason, holding your head. He's a fireman.'

'Hi,' Jason said. 'Must say I'm impressed. It's not everyone that makes sure they've got representatives around from the emergency services when they take their car for a flying lesson.'

'Oh...God,' Bill groaned. 'My car. Is it wrecked?'

'Were you the only person in the car, Bill?' Laura queried.

'Yes. It was just me and that damned dog. The stupid mongrel fell on top of me when I was going around the corner. It's all his fault. I hope he's underneath the car.'

Jason caught Laura's glance but she was glad he didn't voice his obvious reaction to the statement. The 'damned dog' had slithered back to sit on Jason's foot again as soon as Bill had started talking.

'Take a deep breath for me, Bill,' Laura instructed. 'Does anything hurt?'

'No. I'm fine, I said. Let me get up.' Bill tried to move and then swore profusely. 'My leg,' he groaned.

'It's broken,' Laura informed him. 'An ambulance should be here shortly. They'll be able to give you some pain relief.' She could make contact with someone who would give her permission to put an IV line in even though she was off duty, which might speed up the man's analgesia, but Laura's professional empathy for him was much less than it had been before he'd mentioned his dog. 'I'm going to check your neck and back out now,' she told him. 'Try and keep still.'

The new arrival to the scene slithered part way down the bank. 'Your baby's fine,' he called. 'Seems to be sound asleep, and they said the police and ambulance would be here in about ten minutes.'

It was almost an hour later that Jason and Laura finally clambered back up the steep bank as they assisted with carrying Bill's scoop stretcher. He was taken away in the ambulance and a young female police officer reluctantly handed Megan back. 'She was crying,' she explained. 'So I picked her up. She's gorgeous, isn't she?'

Megan was happy enough to go back into her car seat.

'I'll put it in the front seat this time, shall I?' Jason asked. 'I'll sit in the back with Oscar.'

'Are you sure about this?' Laura eyed the fat black dog currently leaning against Jason's leg with its mournful black eyes firmly fixed on his face. 'He doesn't smell great.'

'So we'll give him a bath. We couldn't leave him behind. Bastard Bill was on his way to have him put down.'

'Hmm.' Further conversation had revealed that Bill's mother had gone into a rest home recently and her dog, a six-year-old motley cross between a Labrador and a poodle, had been locked up in Bill's garage because his wife refused to have him in the house. His messy search for food or a distraction in the rubbish bags that morning had been the last straw and Bill had been summoned home from work to deal with it. The SPCA would have been an alternative to having the dog destroyed, but Jason and Oscar had clearly formed a bond.

'A dog is a big responsibility,' Laura felt obliged to remind him. 'Might not be easy keeping one with shift work.'

'Be a darned sight easier than looking after a baby,' Jason declared. 'And kids need a dog around.'

Again, they both ignored the obvious and Jason sat in the back seat with the smelly dog while Laura drove them home. Oscar had to stay outside until later that evening, but as soon as Megan was settled Jason unearthed all the old towels he could find and ran a bath full of warm water.

'Will dishwashing liquid be OK?'

'I think baby shampoo might be better.'

'Hey, good idea! I should have thought of that for *your* bath.'

'You didn't!'

'Didn't what?'

'Put dishwashing liquid in my bath.'

'It needed bubbles. Worked quite well, I thought.'

'No wonder my skin's been feeling so dry all week.'

'Bet it was squeaky clean, though.'

'You're impossible.' Laura laughed. 'But never mind. Let's see if we can get Oscar squeaky clean, shall we?'

Oscar didn't take kindly to being bathed. He shook the offending substance off frequently enough to soak the walls, floor, Jason and Laura. It took six towels to get him reasonably dry, and by then the dog was so tired out by the trauma of it all he curled up on the pile of damp towels and went very firmly to sleep.

'I know how he feels,' Jason groaned. 'I'm heading for bed as soon as I've dried off as well.' He stripped his soaked T-shirt off and was about to drop it on the floor when he caught Laura's stare. She had taken her glasses off because of the rain effect of Oscar's shaking, but even the depth of colour in her brown eyes wasn't enough to conceal the dilation of her pupils. The sight of a pink tongue tip running over her lower lip confirmed what Jason was thinking. The heavy T-shirt slipped from his fingers, unheeded. His mates were right. Laura *did* fancy him.

His gaze didn't stop at her face. Laura's T-shirt was as wet as his had been and it clung to her breasts. Jason dragged his gaze back up to her face and the moment the eye contact was renewed he realised the truth. Any attraction here was mutual. For a long moment they simply stared at each other. And then Jason reached out.

'You'd better get that T-shirt off,' he murmured. 'You'll catch a cold.'

He helped her. It was Jason that dropped the damp garment. This time as their gazes caught Jason was much closer, and it was so easy to bend his head and kiss Laura's upturned face.

One kiss was not enough. It could never have been enough. Jason could taste things he'd never thought it was possible to taste. All the things he liked about Laura were there— her kindness and loyalty, her intelligence and warmth. Her humour and strength. And he learned something new about Laura Green. Despite anything that appearances might have suggested, she was capable of a passion that blew his socks off.

One kiss and then another…and another. Jason's tone when he spoke might have been cheeky but the question in his eyes was very serious.

'I think you might catch a cold, wearing that damp bra. You'd better get it off.'

He helped her. The lacy garment went the same way as the T-shirt and this time Jason could explore the delicious softness of a body type he'd never had the pleasure of tasting before.

'You're gorgeous,' he told Laura. 'Did you know that?'

'You're not half bad yourself,' she responded shyly. Then she caught her bottom lip between her teeth. 'But I think you should get out of those damp jeans before *you* catch a cold.'

She helped him and Jason didn't even bother to stifle a groan of pure desire as she tackled the button and zip. He caught her hands. 'If you want this to stop,' he warned, 'it had better be now.'

The gaze from those chocolate-brown eyes was perfectly steady. 'I don't want it to stop,' she said softly. 'Do you?'

'Hell, no!' Jason grinned, swept Laura up into his arms and carried her towards his bedroom.

For a moment, as she lay on his bed, Jason experienced a flash of panic. Was he out of his mind? This was *Laura*—a mate, one of the boys, no less, and a friend he was depending on to help him through a period of crisis in his life. And then Laura smiled and reached out, drawing his head down to hers, and at the touch of her lips Jason knew he'd never been more sane in his life.

The blinding clarity with which he could suddenly see the reason for all his past romantic disasters was a revelation, drawing a sigh of contentment that mingled with Laura's breath as Jason gave up thinking about the wisdom of what he was doing. Gave up thinking full stop, in fact, and simply allowed himself to experience, body and mind, the most wonderful sex he'd ever had.

The revelation came back later as he lay, curled around Laura's body, listening to her soft, even breathing as she slept. It was as though he'd been trying to fit the pieces of a puzzle together in the wrong order for all these years. Sex, friendship and then a lasting love. It had never worked and now he knew why.

With the friendship and trust coming first, it added a dimension to the sex that he'd never known could exist. Even with Donna, and the twelve-month relationship, by the time they'd developed any kind of trust and friendship, that initial mind-blowing lust had worn off and the friendship had faded in much the same way.

This thing with Laura was completely different. To be honest, it scared the hell out of him because, this time, he didn't want anything to fade. The friendship or the lust. If those held together then he knew that would be the kind of love that could last a lifetime.

He'd told Laura a while back about the attributes he looked for in women. They had to be fun to be with. Adventurous. And at least reasonably intelligent. Laura was fun, no doubt about that, and her intelligence was equally unquestionable. Adventurous? How many women would demand to go slithering down a steep bank to explore a wrecked car for potential victims? Or take on the adoption of a fat, smelly dog? Or move into a virtual stranger's house to help look after a baby, for that matter? What was any of that if it wasn't adventurous?

This was scary all right. Jason could recognise what he'd found and, for the first time in his life, he had found something he really, really didn't want to lose. This was *it*. For all these years he had been skating on the surface of life—all fun and no responsibility. He wouldn't have taken on his current situation if he'd had any real choice in the matter, and he had to admit he wouldn't have looked twice at Laura if he'd been on a mission to find female companionship.

Circumstances had pushed his boundaries and had had the side effect of making Jason grow up a little. He considered the sobering realisation of just how meaningless his love life had been until now. A selection of bimbos who had impressed the hell out of his colleagues, but now he could see himself through Laura's eyes and he almost groaned aloud. No wonder she had told him he was shallow.

He *was* shallow. Or, at least, he had been until now. The depth to which he wanted involvement with Laura was terrifying. She had the power to hurt him very badly if she didn't want what he could offer. And why should she on anything more than a short-term basis? Laura was so far above the kind of women he had always attracted so easily. Maybe she was too good for the likes of him to aspire to.

The fact was that Laura was out of his league in any category that really mattered, and Jason knew it. He'd have to work hard to win her and she wasn't going to settle for second best. She'd walked out on a guy after living with him for two years because he hadn't measured up. Jason couldn't bear the thought of giving all he had and still finding he hadn't made the grade a couple of years down the track.

How could he convince Laura that he was worth being with…for ever?

Darkness hid his smile. He had a bonus that no one else could offer. Something that Laura already loved.

He had Megan.

CHAPTER EIGHT

'WHAT *is* it, Tim?' Laura paused in her task of restocking the resuscitation kit. 'Have I sprouted horns or something?'

'I'm trying to work out what's so different about you.'

'Can't be my hair. I've had it like this for two weeks now.' Laura pushed her fingers through the soft, loose waves framing her face and then shook them back into place. The pleasure of her new, free style had increased rather than worn off. 'We need some more lancets for the blood-glucose kit,' she told Tim. 'And a couple of high-concentration masks.'

'Sure. How's the Entonox cylinder looking, seeing as you're up that end?'

Laura leaned over the end of the stretcher she was sitting on and then laughed as her shirt came adrift from her trousers.

'Oops. I wish my new uniform issue would come through.' She tucked the shirt tail firmly back into place. 'I'm getting sick of these baggy pants.'

'You've lost weight.' Tim nodded slowly. 'Maybe that's it.'

'It's not so much the weight,' Laura told him. 'I've just changed shape a bit. Toned up. It's all the exercise I'm getting.' She leaned more carefully towards the regulator valve of the Entonox cylinder, hoping that Tim wouldn't notice the faint colour she could feel heating her cheeks. Jason had claimed all the credit for keeping her levels of physical activity up enough to burn off a few kilograms. He'd even looked worried.

'You'll turn into a stick insect in six months at this rate. Maybe we should have a night off.'

But they hadn't because neither of them had wanted to. Laura would be quite happy to keep up her steady weight loss but it really didn't matter. She was far happier with the thought of still being with Jason in six months' time.

'It's probably walking Oscar every night that's done the trick.' Laura tried to sound offhand. 'Everybody should adopt a very fat dog when they want to get in shape.'

They both looked out of the window of the ambulance to the fire engine parked beside them in the huge garage. The back passenger window was open and hanging out of it was the curly black head of a happy-looking dog. Oscar had been adopted as readily as Megan had been at the station. He wasn't allowed inside, of course, but even Mrs McKendry had to acknowledge that he was a well-behaved animal. He sat guarding the fire engine during his family's working hours unless it was required for active duty, when he was happy to sleep on the old coat that now had a permanent place on the floor by the locker-room door.

The smile Laura gave on seeing Oscar was imperceptible. Maybe everybody should bathe a very smelly dog when they wanted to kick-start the love affair of their lives. Who would have thought that an unwanted Labradoodle could provide such a romantic catalyst? The dog might have made its intention to worship Jason for the rest of its life obvious by now but he would always have Laura's gratitude and affection. Except possibly when he indulged his passion for exploring rubbish bags.

Laura twisted the key on the regulator and watched the needle flick up the dial. 'Three quarters full,' she informed Tim. 'Enough laughing gas to keep a whole busload of patients happy.'

'*That's* it,' Tim said in a satisfied tone. 'That's what's so different about you. You're happy.'

'I am,' Laura admitted. Happy was a very pale adjective for how she felt but it would do under the circumstances. She was rapt. Her dream had come true. Jason had got to know her well enough to find her attractive and, judging by their love-making over the last two weeks, he found her *very* attractive. And she *felt* attractive, for the first time in her life. The weight loss had very little to do with it. Neither did the new hairstyle. Laura felt wanted and appreciated for far more than what she could offer in bed, and she was loving every minute of it. They had welded into a tight team, she and Jason, and it didn't matter that their focus was so much on Megan—not when they could find the private moments that made every shared sleeping time so memorable.

Laura wouldn't even allow herself the niggling concern that the main reason Jason wanted her to still be there in six months' time might be because he was coming to like the idea of keeping his daughter. She didn't care. She loved both of them too much to let that be a problem. If Jason asked her tomorrow to marry him and be a mother to Megan, she wouldn't hesitate in saying yes.

'Yeah,' Laura said softly, as she caught the look Tim was giving her. Suddenly she wanted to share a little of her joy with her partner. 'I don't think I've ever been this happy before in my life.'

Tim's smile was wistful as he caught her meaning. 'I'm happy *for* you, Laura. You make a wonderful couple. What with Megan and that funny-looking dog you found, you've turned into an instant family.'

Laura watched Tim disappear into the stockroom to find the supplies they needed. The almost imperceptible slump of his shoulders confirmed what she already knew. Her partner wanted a family of his own. He could see the magic that had been wrought in Laura's life and knew that it was never going to happen that easily for him.

It felt exactly like magic. Wave a wand and...*poof*! An instant family. And it was all going so smoothly. They had developed a routine that seemed to work now and most jobs were shared at least to some degree. Megan was settled enough to sleep through the night sometimes, especially since they'd started their long evening walks. The days were getting longer and it was a pleasant way to end the day even after a busy shift. Laura got to hold Oscar's shiny new lead because Jason wore the front pack, which allowed Megan to face forward and view her surroundings, not to mention wave her little arms and kick her legs when things got interesting. She was always tired on their return home and a quick feed and nappy change was usually enough to see her out for the count until morning.

Yes, it felt like a well-oiled family unit. Maybe they would have a problem if Mrs McKendry decided she didn't want to help, but the older woman loved Megan as much as any of them now, and if the worst happened, Laura was quite prepared to consider taking maternity leave to carry on being a surrogate mother.

The fact that Megan was the key to it all shouldn't be enough to cause that niggle of doubt, should it? Or the fact that everything was falling into place so perfectly? OK, so maybe they would have to fight to keep Megan if Shelley decided to come back for her but surely they could win? They'd be a full family unit, complete with a prime example of a contented dog, against a solo mother who'd been prepared to abandon her child.

They could even have the solid base of owning their own home. Laura hadn't yet suggested the idea of moving into *her* house, but it was the logical next step. Charlie had only been intending to live with her until she got settled into her new city and job. Laura had hardly spoken to her in the last couple of weeks and she suspected it had a lot to do with whatever was going on between Charlie and that scary partner she had to work with, so it seemed like she had already settled very well. Laura only hoped that her best friend was half as happy as she was in her love affair. She would never forget the thrill of that first time Jason had said he loved her…not in a million years. Even hearing the echo of his words in her head was enough to create the most delicious tingle that ran the length of her spine.

The latches on the resuscitation kit clicked into place and Laura pushed the box behind the end of the stretcher so it wouldn't cause mischief with fast cornering. She managed to shut off any latent personal worries as her pager sounded to announce a new job. The worst—the very worst—thing that could happen would be that they would lose Megan. It would be hard, awful, but she and Jason could always have children of their own, couldn't they? If Jason lost full-time custody of Megan, he might be very keen to start a family of his own as soon as possible.

It was Tim's turn to drive. Laura was checking the map reference as he pulled the door open, dropped the extra supplies on the floor beside the handbrake and picked up the remote to activate the huge roller doors on the garage.

'Abdo pain,' he said. 'What do you reckon? Appendicitis? Ovarian torsion? Or do we get to deliver a surprise baby for someone this afternoon?'

'It's at a restaurant.' Laura said. 'That posh one on the corner of Frampton and Davies roads. Food poisoning, maybe?'

'Priority one?' Tim activated the beacons and siren as they entered the dense stream of traffic heading into the city centre looking for some Friday night entertainment.

'I imagine the manager of any restaurant would be pretty worried if someone looked sick after eating their food.'

The manager of Framptons looked more than worried. He was waiting on the road for the ambulance and the frantic waving as they approached suggested that the call might be for something rather more serious than food poisoning.

Tim leapt out to open the back doors of the ambulance while Laura slipped out of her seat and straight into the back to start throwing equipment onto the stretcher. They'd take the lot. Life pack, oxygen, resuscitation and suction units. She could hear the restaurant manager's voice as Tim opened the doors.

'She'd finished her meal. They stood up to leave and then she just doubled over, clutching her stomach.'

Tim helped lift the stretcher, laden with gear, to the ground.

'We sat her down and got her a glass of water but she looked terrible.'

They were walking into the restaurant now. Past tables shrouded in crisp, white linen, gleaming silverware and soft, flickering light from small candelabra illuminating bowls of white roses. The venue looked like the perfect setting for a wedding breakfast.

'There was a nurse having dinner at another table. She laid her down on the floor and put her legs up. She started to feel better but then she sat up and kind of fainted.'

'Sounds hypotensive,' Tim commented to Laura.

'Yes, but why?' Waiting staff were hurriedly clearing a route through the dining room, shifting empty chairs and pushing tables together. A group of diners was being moved to a table further away from the scene of the woman's collapse and they stared at the ambulance crew as though they were responsible for the interruption to their meal. Laura ignored the stares. This woman's abdominal pain might actually be epigastric pain from a heart attack. Or something equally serious.

Their patient was lying on the floor near the back corner of the restaurant, a cushion under her head and two more under her feet. An anxious-looking man was holding her hand and a slim, well-dressed blonde woman had her hand on the other wrist.

'Hi,' she said. 'I'm Kathryn Mercer. I'm a nurse.'

'Hi.' Tim's smile was fleeting. 'I'm Tim and this is Laura.'

Laura didn't acknowledge the introduction. The patient looked shocked. She was pale, sweaty and barely conscious. Thankful that she had grabbed one of the high-concentration oxygen masks from the floor, Laura jammed the tubing onto the cylinder outlet. 'What's her name?'

'Jillian,' the man beside her answered.

'Jillian, can you hear me? Open your eyes for me.'

The only response was an incoherent groan.

'No radial pulse,' Tim reported. 'Airway's clear.'

Laura started connecting up the leads for the life pack. A very shiny pair of black shoes appeared behind her elbow and her gaze flicked up for a second, expecting to see the restaurant manager moving in to watch proceedings. The pair of immaculate, pin-striped grey trousers belonged to a stranger, however.

'Come on, Kathryn. It's time we left. There's no need for you to be involved here any longer.'

Tim looked up swiftly from where he was wrapping the blood-pressure cuff around Jillian's arm. He ignored the man in the nice suit. 'How long has she been like this?'

'Only a couple of minutes. She seemed to come right after I got her to lie down and put her feet up. Then she insisted on sitting up and started to look shocked very quickly. Her radial pulse was palpable until her GCS dropped.'

Laura was sticking on electrodes. She heard what seemed to be an exasperated sigh as the shiny shoes disappeared. She paused for just a moment to rub a knuckle on her patient's breastbone. 'Jillian? Open your eyes.'

The response to the painful stimulus was another groan and an uncoordinated attempt to push Laura's hand away, but Jillian's eyes remained closed.

'I'd put the GCS at 7,' Laura said to Tim. She looked up at the other people, her gaze taking in both the nurse, who looked to be about her own age, and Jillian's husband, who was well into his sixties. 'Any medical history?' she queried. 'Does she have a heart condition? Diabetes?'

'She's got high blood pressure,' her husband responded. 'Has done for years. She's not having a stroke, is she? Oh, *God*!' He covered his face with his hands and they could all hear a sob.

The restaurant manager was almost wringing his hands with anxiety and Laura caught his eye. 'Could you take care of Jillian's husband for the moment? It'll be a few minutes before we're ready to leave.'

The manager looked relieved to have a task. He put his arm around the man's heaving shoulders. 'Come with me, sir. Let's get you sitting down just for a minute. Jillian's in the best hands possible right now.'

'It didn't look like a stroke.' Kathryn shook her head. 'She was quite alert earlier and she didn't complain of a headache. I didn't notice any speech difficulties or obvious neurological deficit.'

Tim released the valve on the sphygmomanometer and the air rushed out of the cuff with a hiss. 'BP's 70 over 40,' he reported grimly. 'What's her rhythm like?'

'Sinus,' Laura said. 'Seventy beats per minute.' Oddly normal, in other words.

'I'll get an IV in.' Tim reached into the kit for supplies and Laura picked up a penlight torch and lifted Jillian's eyelids.

'Pupils are equal but both dilated and sluggish.'

'Kathryn.' The clipped word from somewhere behind Laura was a command for attention, but the blonde woman had her gaze fixed on Tim.

'Is there anything else I can do to help?'

'You're a nurse, you said?'

'Yes. I used to work in Emergency, though it's been a while. I'm just a general practice nurse now. Part time.'

'Could you do a blood sugar for us maybe? That is, if...' Tim's raised eyebrow was intended to question the advisability of her staying to help.

'That's fine.' Kathryn raised her head only for a moment. 'Just give me a minute or two, Sean. Please?'

'I'll get a second IV in,' Laura decided. 'She needs fluids, stat. What are you using, a 14 gauge?'

'Yeah. The wider the bore the better right now.'

Kathryn had opened the BGL kit. She held one of the woman's fingers, used the lancet to elicit a drop of blood and then deftly collected the tiny sample on the end of the Glucocard. The meter beeped as it started its calculation.

'You've done that before.' Tim glanced up as he secured a luer plug to the IV cannula he'd just inserted.

'It's one of the few invasive procedures I get to do these days.' The blonde woman's smile was wry. 'I envy you guys.' The meter beeped again and she picked it up. 'BGL's in normal range. It's 5.6.'

'Good. Thanks for that.'

Laura was slipping her cannula into place on Jillian's other arm. 'Could you draw up an extra flush for me, please, Tim?'

'I could do that,' Kathryn offered eagerly.

'Oh, for God's sake.' The irritated snap came from Kathryn's well-dressed partner. 'I've had about enough, Kathryn. Our dinner has already been ruined and now you're making a spectacle of yourself, crawling around on the floor. I'm leaving.' He proved his intention by turning and walking away. 'If you want to stay and play doctors and nurses that's fine, but you'll have to find your own way home.'

Kathryn bit her lip, hesitated fractionally but then scrambled to her feet. 'OK, Sean. I'm coming.' Hurriedly, she reached down to grab an empty syringe packet and a pen. She scribbled down a telephone number.

'Could you...? I mean, would you mind ringing me, please?' she asked Tim. 'To let me know how she gets on?'

'Sure.'

Kathryn turned but walked only a step or two before turning back. 'What do you think it *is*?' she asked quietly. 'An MI?'

Tim shook his head. 'She's presented with acute abdo pain, rapid deterioration to shock and she's hypotensive but hasn't developed a rise in her heart rate. My pick is a dissecting or ruptured aortic aneurysm.'

'I think you're right,' Laura said seconds later as Kathryn vanished through the front door of the restaurant. 'There's no palpable femoral pulse on the left side.'

'BP's coming up.' Tim pulled the stethoscope from his ears. 'Let's see if we need to get some morphine on board and then we'd better load and go.'

An hour later, Laura was again restocking the resuscitation kit. She removed empty packaging and a full sharps container so she could see what was missing. 'Amazing how much of a mess we can make, dealing with a medical emergency.'

'Great job, though, wasn't it?' Tim sounded happy. 'And we were right. It was a dissecting aneurysm. I'll wait till she comes out of Theatre and then ring Kathryn to tell her about it.'

'She's been lucky,' Laura said. 'If she hadn't been so close to a hospital she would have been in serious trouble.'

Tim didn't appear to be listening. He was hunting in his pockets. 'You didn't throw that package away, did you? The one with her phone number?' He tried his shirt pocket and sighed with relief. 'No, here it is.'

Laura bit her lip. She had never seen Tim look rattled about something so minor. 'So you're going to call her, then?'

'Are you kidding? The woman of my dreams just gave me her phone number and *asked* me to call her.'

'But, Tim…' Laura frowned. 'She wasn't exactly alone.'

'I don't think she liked her dinner date any more than anyone else did. What a jerk, complaining about having his meal interrupted because Kathryn's trying to help someone who's seriously sick.'

'But…' Laura cleared her throat. 'She was wearing a wedding ring, Tim. So was he.'

'Was she?' Animation died from Tim's face. 'How on earth did you have time to notice that?'

Laura shrugged. Maybe her subconscious was tuned to noticing things pertaining to weddings at present. Like the silver and white theme in the restaurant. And the plain gold bands on other people's fingers. After all, her dream of Jason putting one on her own finger was a great deal closer than it had been a month ago. Tim turned away with a sigh.

'Why am I not surprised?' he muttered. He screwed up the packaging and dropped it onto the little pile Laura had collected. 'Even if she wasn't married, she probably wouldn't have been interested. I hope you realise how lucky you are, Laura.'

'Oh, I do, don't worry,' Laura murmured. She felt sorry for Tim but his turn would come one of these days. He was a lovely guy and he deserved the same kind of happiness she had found. One that would last a lifetime.

A couple of days might be a lifetime for some kind of insect but it was the blink of an eye for Laura Green. And when she answered the late-evening knock on the front door of Jason's house in Crighton Terrace, she knew instantly that she was in trouble.

If she had collated everything she knew about Jason Halliday and invented a prototype for what he would consider to be the perfect woman, the embodiment of that ideal was currently standing on his doorstep. She didn't need to introduce herself, but that didn't stop those perfectly painted pink lips from opening. Laura had a wild urge to slam the door shut in her face. Instead, she simply waited for the inevitable.

'Hi, I'm Shelley Bates.' Laura found herself stepping back in response to the visitor's forward movement rather than any desire to issue an invitation. 'Is Jason home?'

The nerve of the woman! She actually brushed past Laura as though she were some kind of maid and then walked confidently up the hallway to enter the living room. Laura saw the colour leach from Jason's face as she followed Shelley. He glanced at Laura and the pain of betrayal seemed to be directed at her. It wasn't fair!

'She just waltzed in, Jase. I couldn't stop her.'

Shelley dropped a carry bag, which was large enough to appear ominous, beside the couch. Large blue eyes were regarding Jason. 'I'm sorry to drop in without any warning,' she said, 'but I couldn't bear to be away from Meggie a moment longer.'

Jason's jaw sagged. 'Who are you trying to kid?' he said incredulously. 'You dumped your baby on a doorstep and took off. Well, you can just take off again now as far as we're concerned. We don't want you here.'

Laura hadn't realised she was holding her breath until she felt it seeping out now. 'That's right,' she said coolly. 'Jason is more than capable of caring for his daughter.'

'So you do accept that she's yours?' Shelley smiled for the first time and Laura stared at the perfect teeth in the perfect face. 'I'm so pleased, Jason. I wasn't sure that you would.'

'So that was why you decided to dump her?' Jason hadn't returned the smile. His face was set grimly and the hold on the baby in his arms had tightened enough to make Megan squeak softly in surprise.

'Yes,' Shelley said surprisingly. 'I knew if *I* turned up with the baby you would have no problem in ignoring both of us. Denying fatherhood and simply sending us packing. I knew my only chance was to make sure you had the opportunity to get to know and accept your daughter.'

Only chance for what? Laura stood beside Jason, stony-faced.

'And now? I suppose you think you can just take her away as easily as you brought her.' Jason cleared his throat. 'You might have bitten off a bit more than you can chew, Shelley.'

'I have no intention of taking her away from you.' Shelley walked towards where they were standing. Oscar raised his head from where it was resting on Jason's knee and growled softly. 'She looks very happy.' Shelley peered over the edges of the blanket and her blue eyes became very bright. 'Hello, darling,' she crooned. 'Mummy's missed you *so* much.'

Laura felt a faint wave of nausea. Surely Jason could see how fake this woman was? He didn't appear to have thawed yet.

'What do you intend to do, then, Shelley?'

Go back to England, Laura wanted to suggest tartly. Get the hell out of our lives and stay out.

'I just want to talk, Jason. We've got a lot to talk *about*, haven't we?'

'I suppose so.' The agreement was grudging. 'I guess you'd better sit down.'

Shelley didn't move. She looked directly at Laura for the first time since entering the house. 'It really is a private matter.'

'I don't have any secrets from Laura,' Jason responded. 'And she's as involved in all this as any of us.'

'Really?' Shelley's glance was almost amused. As competition, Laura had just been summarily dismissed.

Seething inwardly, Laura sat on an armchair. Shelley sat on the couch but Jason remained standing, the baby in his arms, the dog pressed firmly against his leg.

Laura watched the longest, most elegant legs she had ever seen cross themselves and display a significant amount more thigh. No matter how toned or thin she herself became, she would never possess legs like that without some kind of transplant. Then Shelley reached up to flick long blonde hair over one shoulder and the movement raised her short top enough to reveal a flat belly with a glinting jewel in her navel. A glance at Jason revealed his gaze was riveted to the woman on the couch and

Laura felt something cold and hard form inside her.

He was attracted to Shelley. What man wouldn't be? And Shelley Bates had a card Laura could never play. She was Megan's birth mother. She could take Jason's now beloved child away from him…or she could use her to pull Jason back into her life.

Which was clearly what her intention was.

'I've never forgotten you, Jason. It was the most wonderful holiday I've ever had and the night with you was the best part.'

'You could have fooled me. You didn't even bother to meet me at that pub the next night.'

So, Jason had wanted it to be a little more than a one-night stand, had he? Megan made a distressed noise that fitted how Laura was feeling remarkably well. At least the baby's discomfort could be eased, however.

'I'll fix her a bottle, shall I?'

'I couldn't,' Shelley told Jason. 'We'd taken a boat trip out to Slipper Island and the weather got rough. We had to stay overnight and when I went looking for you the next day, you had gone. I had no idea how to get hold of you.' The sigh was heartfelt. 'I tried again when I found out I was pregnant, of course, but all I knew was your name and that you were a fireman. You wouldn't think New Zealand was a big enough country to make it difficult to find out where someone lives, would you?'

'No,' Jason said. Megan cried again, more loudly this time, and Laura simply got up and walked to the kitchen.

'After Megan was born my b-brother decided he had to help.'

What was that stammer about? Laura wondered sourly, as she stirred formula. Had she just managed to modify 'boyfriend' into something acceptable in time? It hadn't been a 'brother' Mrs Mack had seen delivering the box to the station's doorstep. And where was he now, anyway? She went back into the sitting room a few minutes later and silently handed the bottle to Jason.

'Thanks.' The smile Laura received was distracted, however. Jason's attention was firmly directed to the woman on the couch. 'Where have you been for the last month, Shelley?''

'Just travelling,' she responded sadly, watching as Jason sat down in the armchair and arranged the baby and bottle into satisfactory positions. 'I was in Dunedin most of the time. My brother, Darryn, has a friend there who's trying to find a job. I was just filling in time, thinking about you and Megan and wondering whether you would learn to love her if you were given the chance.'

The longer the silence that fell ticked on, the more significant it seemed to become. Finally, Jason cleared his throat.

'Yeah…well, I guess it worked.'

Shelley's huge blue eyes radiated joy. 'That's wonderful. Now all we need to do is plan our future.'

'*Our* future?' Jason's incredulity echoed the word that was sounding a strident alarm in Laura's head.

'We have a baby, Jason,' Shelley told him softly. 'The result of the love we shared.'

'For one night,' Jason reminded her. 'It was sex, not love, Shelley.'

'For you, maybe. I think it was more than that. I've never forgotten that night, and I've never forgotten *you*.'

Laura could understand that, even if she still wasn't at all convinced of this woman's sincerity. If she'd only ever had a single night with Jason, it would be burned into her memory banks for ever as well.

'I want my baby to have a father,' Shelley whispered. 'I want her to have *her* father.'

'I have no intention of abandoning my daughter.'

'But I want her to have a real father. Not someone on the other side of the world.'

'I'm not planning to shift to Britain,' Jason said firmly. 'But Megan can stay here. I'm sure she'll be allowed to stay in the country on a permanent basis once I'm legally registered as her father.'

'But *I* wouldn't be allowed to stay,' Shelley said softly. 'And my daughter is staying with me.'

Stick had hit the nail right on the head, Laura realised. Shelley Bates was out to emigrate and Megan was the ace she hadn't bothered to keep up her sleeve. If Jason wanted to keep Megan in his life, he was going to have to marry her mother. And that wouldn't be too much of a hardship, would it?

Shelley was obviously too clever to push the point right now. Instead, she stood up, walked towards Jason and held out her arms.

'I think it's time I got to hold my baby, isn't it?'

For a long second, time seemed to stop. *Don't give her Megan*, Laura pleaded silently. *If you hand her over then she's already won.* Then Shelley wiped away a tear that was trickling slowly down the side of her nose.

'Please, Jason?'

The lone tear had done the trick. Laura watched the conflict play across Jason's face. Should he do what he wanted to do and hold onto his child or create further suffering for the woman who was, in all fairness, Megan's mother? Slowly, grudgingly, he transferred his bundle.

To Laura's immense satisfaction, Megan took one look at her mother and started howling.

'Oh, I know, darling.' Shelley clutched the baby and rocked her back and forth. 'Mummy's sorry she left you. But I'm back now. Everything's going to be fine.'

Laura looked at her. She looked at the overnight bag beside the couch. She looked at Megan. And she looked at Jason, who wasn't looking back at her.

Everything was *not* going to be fine but there was very little Laura could do about it. She had competition now for what she wanted

most in her life and while she would be prepared to fight if she knew she had any chance
of winning, the odds were rapidly stacking
against her.

Even Megan seemed to be letting her down
as her cries died away. Shelley continued rocking her and another tear rolled down her cheek.

'I don't know how I've lasted this long
without her,' she sighed. 'She was all I had
left that really mattered.' She looked up
through dewy lashes to smile brokenly at
Jason. 'I have a lot to thank you for.'

He simply raised an eyebrow. An unwanted
pregnancy for a teenager wasn't usually a
cause for celebration.

'When Sharon died I felt so terribly alone,'
Shelley continued softly. 'To lose a sister is
bad enough but being a twin made it unbearable.'

'What happened to Sharon?' Jason sounded
disconcerted.

'She had a blood clot that they said was
caused by her being on the Pill. It caused a
massive pull…pum…something that wrecked
her lungs.'

'Pulmonary embolism?' Laura suggested.

'That's it.' Shelley didn't bother to look at Laura. Her gaze was still fixed on Jason. 'She was put on the waiting list for a heart-lung transplant but it didn't come in time.'

Jason's face softened noticeably. 'That must have been rough.'

Shelley nodded and Laura closed her eyes. Jason was starting to feel sorry for Megan's mother. Any judgmental attitude was undergoing reconsideration. She could almost feel another chunk of the fantasy future she'd been building being ripped away.

'When did it happen?'

'She lived just long enough to see Megan. To...hold her.' Shelley's lip quivered and she struggled to maintain control. 'It was Sharon who chose her name. And she made me promise that I would try to find you and give her a real family. She said my life...and her baby's had to go on, and what better way to make a new start than in a new country?'

Jason's expression plainly revealed the level of sympathy she would expect from someone as kind as he was. The story had touched him deeply, which was hardly surprising. Even Laura could feel a lump the size of a small boulder lodged in her own throat. How factual this story was didn't matter a damn. Shelley had just cracked any barrier Jason had in place and it was only a matter of time before she broke through completely.

Megan must have sensed the tension in the atmosphere because she began crying again.

'I'll have to go soon,' Shelley said. 'I've got nowhere to stay in Wellington so I'll have to find a motel or something.' She looked around. 'Is Meggie's blanket here somewhere?'

'You're not planning to take Megan to some motel, are you?' Laura was horrified.

'She's *my* baby.'

'You're not taking Megan anywhere,' Jason told her firmly. 'Not until we get a few things sorted out.'

'I'll have to stay here, then. I'm not going without her and I'm too tired to talk any more tonight.'

Megan hiccuped, then burped and then her crying stopped. The silence stretched on even longer this time. Laura tried desperately to make eye contact with Jason to warn him not to fall into the trap, but he was avoiding her gaze.

'I suppose you could have Mitch's room for a night or two,' Jason conceded at last. He looked at Laura finally, a plea of his own written across his face. But Laura wasn't prepared to go along with this. Megan might be this woman's child but it just felt *wrong* to see the baby in her arms. She couldn't stay in the same house as Shelley Bates.

'It's time I went home for a night or two, anyway.'

'What?'

'I think Shelley's right. This is something the two of you need to sort out.' She couldn't bear sitting here like a piece of the furniture, watching her future unravel before her eyes. It was simply too painful.

'You can't just walk out.' Jason followed her to the door a short time later. 'What the hell am I supposed to do with Shelley?'

'It was you that invited her to stay, Jase.'

'Only because I don't want her dragging Megan off to go hunting for a place to sleep.'

Laura shook her head. 'You don't need me here. I think you've got more chance of dealing with all this if I'm *not* here. You've got the rest of tonight and all day tomorrow to try and sort things out with Shelley.'

'I don't know how to sort things out.'

'You need to decide what you want and don't let her manipulate you into anything else.'

'I want you to stay.'

'What about Megan?'

'I don't know,' Jason said miserably. 'I know Shelley's her mother but something doesn't feel right.'

Laura said nothing. Of course it didn't feel right. Any concern Shelley had for her child was blatantly fake. Jason, however, had developed a very genuine bond with his daughter and if he decided that Shelley wasn't going to give Megan the love and security she deserved then he would do whatever it took to put things right. And of course he wanted Laura to stay. If he did end up keeping Megan, he would never manage on his own, would he?

Love came in so many shades. Laura knew that Jason was perfectly sincere in telling her he loved her, but did his love come anywhere near measuring up to the depth of her feelings for him? John used to say he loved her often enough when what he really loved was having someone around to love *him*.

Laura suddenly felt very, very tired. If Jason didn't feel as strongly as she did right now, he never would, and she was not going to spend the rest of her life trying to earn a love that came anywhere near being reciprocal.

Megan was the key to all of this. The magic had begun with her unexpected arrival in their lives and now reality was kicking back in and choices had to be made. Jason had accepted responsibility for his daughter. Now he had to take responsibility for making those choices.

Laura knew she could never happily accept a future that didn't contain Jason. Now it was time to find out whether he felt the same way about her, and the only way that could happen was if she stepped back.

Standing on tiptoe, Laura planted a soft kiss on Jason's lips. 'Good luck.'

'I'll need it.' The last glimpse of his face as the door closed showed an expression as grim as his tone.

But it wasn't Jason who needed the luck, it was Laura. And she had a horrible feeling that she had used up more than her fair share already in the last month. The fairy dust had well and truly worn off.

CHAPTER NINE

FOR once, the baby's whimper at 5 a.m. came as a relief.

Jason rolled from his bed, tightened the frayed cord supporting his pyjama pants and reached into the nearby bassinet. At the touch of his hands, Megan fell silent. As Jason picked up his daughter, she smiled at him.

'I don't think you're *that* hungry, are you?'

Knowing that Shelley was in the house made Jason reluctant to leave his room. He had transferred the bassinet in here last night, and closing the door firmly had given him a sense of safety. His own space to consider developments in the company of the things that had become most important to him.

Shelley had simply shrugged when he said he'd keep Megan in his room. 'I guess you know where all the nappies and bottles are,' she'd said. 'We'll sort all that out tomorrow.'

She might have raised an objection if she'd seen Oscar slipping through the gap before the door closed, but the dog was now part of the family as far as Jason was concerned, and his family needed protection. Laura should have been here as well. Jason eyed the empty bed and scowled.

How could she have packed a bag and deserted him at a time of crisis like this? Maybe he'd been wrong to feel he could trust her with his life. Maybe she wasn't as strong as he'd thought. The going had got tough and Laura had got going in the direction of the nearest available exit.

With a deep sigh, Jason climbed back into his bed with Megan still in his arms. He pushed Oscar with his foot to make some more space.

'You won't get away with sleeping there when Laura comes home again, mate.'

Except she *had* gone home, hadn't she? This wasn't her home. She'd only been here because of Megan, and now Megan's mother had returned to lay claim to her baby. No wonder Laura had left. Jason closed his eyes on a wave of misery. He'd been wrong in thinking that Megan might be the ace up his sleeve in his determination to keep Laura in his life on a permanent basis. Perhaps she was the *only* real draw card and if he lost his daughter then he would lose Laura as well. What did he have to offer apart from his daughter, anyway?

A reputation as a shallow Casanova, that was what. With an excellent specimen of the kind of woman that had populated his past right here in his house at present. He had a career with awkward shift hours that could put pressure on a long-term relationship and a house that he would have trouble affording the whole rent on if he had to support a family. Laura seemed to like the sex but the kind of passion they had been sharing for the last couple of weeks couldn't last, could it? Jason knew from repeated personal experience that good sex wasn't nearly enough.

'You've got soggy pants,' he told Megan. He poked her tummy gently. 'Do you want some clean ones?'

Megan reached out and caught his forefinger with her hand, still so tiny that his finger looked ridiculously huge. Jason felt his eyes prickle as he watched the little starfish hand curl into a miniature fist with his finger locked firmly in its centre. Dammit—he'd had no sleep and too much to think about and his physical and mental exhaustion was turning him into a girl.

'Not that there's anything wrong with being a girl,' he said aloud, apologetically. Megan beamed up at him and Jason groaned inwardly.

'You're not making this any easier, you know.' With another sigh, Jason gave in and smiled back.

'The way I see it, Peanut,' he continued softly, 'I haven't got a chance of getting what I really want out of all this. If I get to keep you, I get your mum in the picture as well, and that's not going to make Laura very happy. If I don't get to keep you then I probably won't get to keep Laura either. And...' Jason's voice dropped to a whisper. 'I really like Laura, you know? She's warm and funny and kind and very, very clever and...'

Jason's gaze drifted to the empty side of his bed. Megan's ears were way too young to hear about how he could never get tired of Laura's soft, delicious body and the way it responded to his. He'd never go for a skinny chick again. No way.

Hell, he didn't want to have to even think about going for anyone else.

He wanted Laura. So much that it hurt. Another smile from Megan twisted the knife in his gut. He also loved this tiny person he was holding. A very different kind of love but just as strong in its own way. Or was it so very different? He got the same feeling of responsibility for their health and happiness, the same fierce desire to protect them. Even the disreputable canine currently sprawled over his feet elicited an echo of that feeling. They had all become a family and Jason was learning the hard way that a family was a valuable asset rather than the liability he'd always feared.

A squeak from Megan interrupted the spiral of thoughts Jason had spent the night revisiting.

'You *do* need breakfast, don't you?' Jason eased his foot out from under Oscar's rump. 'And clean pants.' Pins and needles assaulted his foot as it made contact with the floor. 'Come on, then, guys.'

It was still dark but the dawn chorus of birdsong could be heard starting up. Jason flicked on a lamp and moved quietly in the dim light as he prepared a bottle, the weight of the baby on one arm a now familiar and easy burden to cope with. It was a little harder to test the temperature of the milk one-handed so Jason waited until he was settled onto one end of the couch.

'Sh...sh...sh,' he soothed Megan, whose cries rose demandingly when she caught sight of the bottle as he sprinkled milk on his wrist. 'OK, it's just right. Here you go, sweetheart.'

Megan sucked hungrily, making a contented grunting sound at the same time. Jason watched, letting himself relax for the first time in hours and simply enjoying the moment instead of agonising over the complications his life now contained. Things would sort themselves out somehow.

They had to.

Oscar raised his head from Jason's foot a minute or two later, floppy black ears pricked forward and the faint rumble of a growl coming from deep within the shaggy chest. Glancing up, Jason felt a rush of adrenalin tightening his muscles and wiping out any sense of relaxation.

'Hi.' Shelley was wearing a tiny singlet top with shoestring straps that left her belly and half her breasts exposed. The silk boxer shorts that sat low on her hips did nothing to conceal long, tanned legs. 'Can I help?'

'We're fine, thanks.' Jason had to clear his throat. There was no denying that Shelley was an extremely attractive young woman. It was all too easy to remember exactly what had led to their fateful night together. It had probably been all too easy for Laura to understand as well, Jason realised. He could only hope that Laura didn't think he was still attracted, at least on anything more than an 'enjoying the eye candy' basis.

'It's very early.' Jason turned his gaze back to the infant he was holding. 'Why don't you go back to bed for a while?'

Shelley said nothing and Jason felt the air in the room stir as she moved towards him. With fluid grace, she sat down and then curled her legs up beneath her on the other side of the couch. He looked up to see her head tilted provocatively to one side.

'I will if you come with me.'

Jason swallowed hard. He could think of a great many men who would kill to be in his position right now, but it was totally wasted on him. He shouldn't have offered Shelley a place to stay, but then he'd thought at the time that Laura would be here as well. He'd only offered because he hadn't wanted to antagonise Shelley. They had things to sort out and Jason wanted that sorting out to be to his advantage. Their advantage. His *and* Laura's.

Thanks to Laura's defection, he was now going to have to avoid antagonising Shelley on a much more delicate issue. What was to stop her taking Megan and simply disappearing? Jason could imagine with how little urgency any authorities would view tracking down a child he hadn't known even existed until a month ago and who was now back with its birth mother. Jason's hold on Megan tightened imperceptibly. He was going to have to make sure that he kept both Megan and Shelley in sight at all times, so it probably was a good thing that she'd wanted to stay.

'Well?' Shelley ran the tip of her tongue across her upper lip. 'What do you say, Jason? For old times' sake, maybe?'

'I don't think that would be a good idea, Shelley.' It was hard to believe he was looking at the same woman who had been over-whelmed by grief for her twin sister only hours ago. There was no hint of any lingering distress now.

'*I* do.' Shelley uncurled her legs and suddenly she was kneeling beside him on the couch. She pushed her fingers into his tousled hair and her lips tickled his ear as she spoke very softly. '*I* think it would be a lovely idea.'

The touch of her tongue in his ear was too much. Jason stood up. 'Megan's finished her milk,' he said hurriedly. 'She needs burping.'

Shelley sprawled on the couch, gazing up at him. The faint narrowing of her eyes faded and she smiled. 'You want me, Jason. You know you do.'

Jason shook his head. 'I'm in a relationship now,' he told her. 'One that means a lot. I'm not going to cheat on Laura.'

The snort from Shelley was contemptuous. 'What's she got that I couldn't give you, Jason?' She sat up. 'More importantly, what have I got to give you that she hasn't?'

Jason said nothing. He rubbed Megan's back and felt like he was soothing himself as well as the baby. The burp she produced would have made Stick proud, and Jason smiled lop-sidedly as he saw Shelley roll her lovely blue eyes with disgust. So much for all her protestations in front of Laura about how much she loved and had missed Megan.

'You're not really into babies, are you, Shelley?'

'She was an unexpected little gift,' Shelley said smoothly. 'But I love her far too much to part with her now.'

'Why did you decide to go through with the pregnancy?' Jason asked bluntly.

Shelley licked her lips but it was a far from sensual action. It looked more like nervousness. 'I…um…I didn't realise until it was too late.'

'So you didn't want a baby, then.'

'Of course not. I'm only twenty, Jason. I've got my whole life ahead of me.'

'Of course you have.' Jason was quite happy to sound sympathetic again. 'It's far too young to be tied into parenthood.'

Shelley nodded. 'It's not that I don't love Megan,' she added.

'She's a lovable baby all right,' Jason agreed.

'So you want to keep her?'

'Yes.' A simple word. Why did it have the effect of making Jason's heart skip and a prickle of perspiration break out down the length of his spine?

'You can keep her,' Shelley said softly. 'She can be yours, Jason.'

'In return for?'

'Marrying me.'

'*What?*' Jason stared at Shelley. 'Are you crazy?'

'No.' Shelley shook her hair back from her face and her expression hardened. 'Look, you don't have to sleep with me if you don't want to. Though I'm sure that's only a matter of time.' Her gaze flicked up and down the length of Jason's body. 'I've no objections.'

Jason wished he was wearing more than his pyjama bottoms. He also vowed never to look at a woman again in a way that could be construed as sizing up their potential performance in bed. It didn't feel like he was being appreciated. It was downright degrading, but he managed to keep the 'in your dreams' comment silent.

'You'll have to live with me, though,' Shelley said calmly. 'And make it look like more than a marriage in name only. And it'll have to last long enough for me to get my permanent resident's status. That will take a year or so after you agree to sponsor me and make an application to the immigration department.'

'You've got it all worked out, haven't you?'

'I know what I want.' Shelley stood up and walked towards the door. 'And I intend to get it. I'm sure that fat girlfriend of yours will understand. She can live with us too, if she wants. We could use a nanny.'

She turned as she reached the door. 'The alternative is that I take Megan back to England and you never see either of us ever again. I might have her adopted, and it will probably be at least twenty years before you manage to track her down. Your choice, Jason. Have a think about it. I'm going back to bed.'

'I don't know what to do.'

'How about drinking that coffee before it's stone cold?'

'I mean, I'd love to just kick her out, but she says that if she goes then Megan goes with her.' Jason picked up his coffee mug but then put it down without drinking from it. 'She doesn't give a damn about Megan. OK, she might have got up at five a.m. yesterday but helping to feed a baby wasn't what she had in mind.'

'Oh?' Laura felt the cold, hard knot in her stomach grow a little heavier. 'Did she try and seduce you, Jase?'

Jason shook his head but it was a movement of disgust rather than denial. 'She's making a big mistake if she thinks she can use sex to get what she wants.'

Laura stared into the remaining liquid at the bottom of her own coffee mug. Shelley was probably very successful in using sex to get exactly what she wanted. Just how far had the attempted seduction gone? Laura felt sick. It wasn't as if she had any real claim on Jason. She was an aberration in his normal lifestyle as far as women were concerned, and she had won her place purely because of Megan's presence. How long would it take for Jason to revert to type with that kind of temptation laid out on a plate?

'What are you going to do, Jase?'

'I don't know,' Jason said miserably. 'It's really doing my head in.' He glanced at the baby sleeping peacefully in the car seat beside his chair, then his gaze took in the rest of the kitchen and the small adjoining living area. 'This is a really nice little house, Laura. Could Megan and I stay here with you for a few days, maybe?'

'What would that solve?'

'It would get me away from Shelley. Give me some time to think of what to do. She's so bloody determined to get what she wants and I can't talk any sense into her.'

What Shelley wanted was Jason. And Jason clearly wasn't prepared to risk losing his child if he could find a way to keep her.

'Have you spoken to a solicitor? Asked about trying to get custody?'

'No.' Jason pushed his fingers through his hair in a frustrated gesture that created spikes in the blond-streaked waves. 'That would antagonise her right now. I've made it bad enough by saying I'm not prepared to marry her.'

'She wants you to *marry* her? Just like that?'

Jason nodded unhappily. 'She's been quite upfront about it. She wants to live in New Zealand and marriage is the easiest ticket to permanent residency. She says if I don't marry her she'll go back to England and I'll never see Megan again. She's threatened to have her adopted so I can't even trace where she is. I don't know what the adoption laws in England are like but I'm not going to find out by letting that happen.'

Laura could feel the tension in her jaw as she unconsciously gritted her teeth. Shelley was some kind of monster. How could anyone play with a child's life like that? And this wasn't just any baby. This was *Megan* they were talking about.

Jason caught Laura's gaze. 'She also says it doesn't have to be a real marriage. As long as we live together and make it *look* real. She's even got that planned out. She reckons that big old house on the corner of the street would be cheap and I could do it up on my days off. Then we could sell it for a great profit, get divorced and everyone would be happy.'

Laura held his gaze long enough to let him know just how happy such a plan would make her. Jason's smile was grim.

'She even said she doesn't mind if you live with us.'

Laura snorted. 'What as, the nanny?'

His embarrassment was a dead give-away. The fact that Jason was even considering Shelley's proposition enough to repeat it let Laura know how right she had been in thinking she didn't have a hope of winning this competition. She only had a small window of hope that she might be a lot more than a nanny as far as Jason was concerned. With her heart beating a tattoo, Laura tried to find a reason to hang onto that hope.

'Keeping Megan is what matters most, isn't it?' Please, Laura thought desperately. Tell me that *I'm* just as important. That it wouldn't be the complete end of the world if you didn't get to keep your daughter.

'I don't think I could live with myself if I let Shelley take her. What if she just abandoned her again? Left her on the doorstep of some orphanage or something?'

Or, worse, kept her in a home where she was unloved and unwanted. Laura could feel the sharp need to take responsibility herself, and Megan wasn't even her own child. She had to admire Jason for the depth of his caring, and she knew that what he said was right...but it wasn't exactly reassuring her of any priority she herself might have in his life.

Jason seemed to take her silence as support. 'You understand how I feel about this, don't you, Laura? I mean, you love her too, don't you?'

'You know I do, Jase.'

'And we love each other.' The smile was a pale shadow of the usual winning variety but the clasp of Jason's hand was warm and strong. 'I *do* love you, Laura.'

'I love you, too,' she whispered.

'And I need you.' The squeeze on her hand was gently persuasive. 'So does Megan. You, me and Megan. We could be a real family…for ever.' Jason was still smiling. 'So how 'bout it, babe? Would *you* marry me?'

It wasn't really a proposal, was it? Jason was just testing a possible scenario, wasn't he? His next words vaporised any thrill that Laura hadn't been able to suppress.

'I mean, if *we* were married, we'd have a great case for going for permanent custody of Megan.' Jason looked around again. 'And this is such a great house. You own it, don't you?'

'Yes.' Laura swallowed hard. She had a lot going for her, didn't she? 'I'm sharing it with Charlie at the moment, though.'

'Your best friend, right? The serious crash investigator?'

Laura pulled her hand away from Jason's. It hadn't been difficult to distract Jason from any thoughts of proposing marriage, had it? Laura couldn't bear trying to analyse why that might be the case. Changing the subject was probably a wise move.

'Did you hear about the mass casualty incident up north yesterday?' Her voice sounded oddly high pitched so Laura cleared her throat and tried again. 'The train v. bus?'

'It was all over the news. Wish I'd been there. Once-in-a-lifetime opportunity, working on a job that big.'

'Huge,' Laura agreed. 'Charlie and her partner got sent up to help.'

'So she's away?' Jason looked hopeful. 'You do have room for a visitor or two, then?'

'She's back tonight. And you can't just run away from this, Jason. It's got to be sorted. Where is Shelley now?'

'I dropped her off in town.' Jason shook his head. 'She didn't get up until eleven and she didn't bother even holding Megan before telling me she needed to go and meet her brother off the bus from Dunedin. They're planning to check the availability of flights back to the UK. Apparently neither of them have enough money to stay much longer.'

'She's putting the pressure on, then, isn't she?'

'You're not kidding.' Jason checked his watch. 'I'd better head off. With a bit of luck I'll get some time to myself and a chance to try and get my head straight. My guess is that this brother of Shelley's will be wanting a place to stay tonight as well. I'm going to have to try and talk sense into both of them so I need to figure out how I'm going to do it.'

'Good luck.'

'Are you sure you won't come and stay? Help me convince them?'

Laura shook her head sadly. 'It would only make things more difficult, Jase. Shelley's after you, despite pretending she'd be happy with a ''name only'' marriage. If I'm around, she's only going to be more determined to get exactly what she wants.'

Laura had to hold back tears as Jason kissed her goodbye. The kiss was tender but it eased the look of frustration and misery on Jason's features only momentarily.

'I miss having you around,' he said sadly. 'So does Megan.'

Laura looked away. She wanted so much to hold him, to tell him that she loved him and would be there for him no matter what, but she knew what was holding her back. She was desperate for any clue that what they had together was precious for its own sake and not just because it bonded them into a set of parents for Megan.

'Are you managing OK...with Megan?'

'Oh, sure.' Jason's smile was as tender as his kiss had been. 'You've taught me a lot, Laura.'

The tears were much harder to control now. Impossible, in fact. Laura held the door open and her voice was muffled.

'Are you coming into work tomorrow?'

'Of course. I'm going to need a day away from my unwelcome visitors.' Jason managed a lopsided grin. 'Besides, Mackie would have my guts for garters if she missed out on a day with Peanut.'

Jean McKendry wasn't thrilled with the offer of help to care for Megan the next day.

'What does she think she's doing? She made a right pig's ear of changing the bairn's nappy.'

'I guess she's out of practice.'

'She's never been in practice, if you ask me.' The sniff was scathing. 'Why doesn't she just go back where she came from?'

Laura turned to look at Shelley, sitting in the far corner of the commonroom, flicking the pages of a magazine. She smiled as she caught an audible muttering from Mrs Mack concerning the desirable location of a great many Sassenachs.

'The problem is that she wants to take Megan back with her.' Laura kept her voice as low as the whole conversation had been. 'And Jason isn't prepared to let her.'

'I should think not,' Jean hissed. 'She's no fit mother for the likes of our wee bairn.'

Shelley must have been able to feel the heat of the glare she was receiving. She sent back an 'oh, *whatever!*' expression and returned to her magazine with an audible and very bored sigh.

'She'll get sick of sitting around here, pretending to be interested in being a mother.'

'I hope so,' Laura murmured. The novelty of having Shelley on station might wear off for the rest of Green Watch as well. Despite even more obvious support for Jason and Laura than Maxine's visit had inspired, there was no getting away from the fact that the men found Shelley astonishingly attractive.

Stick had been seen to poke Jason hard in the ribs as they'd left for their first callout that morning. 'Didn't you say she had an identical twin sister? Bring it on, mate!'

'You don't want to go there,' Jason responded.

'Are you kidding?'

'She's dead, mate.' Jason's voice had faded as the door swung shut. 'But you're welcome to the one that's left. She's dead keen on finding a New Zealand husband. Be my guest.'

Jean McKendry's attitude took a turn for the worse that afternoon. Waves of righteous indignation met both Jason and Laura when they arrived back from separate jobs at almost the same time.

'She just left her lying on the couch and walked off.'

'Where did she go?'

'Last I saw was her getting on a bus at the stop across the road. That's when I went to check on Megan and found the puir lassie just lying on the couch.'

Jason looked worried. 'Thank goodness she didn't take Megan with her. We're going to have to keep a closer eye on her when she comes back.'

'I hope she's no' coming back at all,' Jean snapped. 'That bairn could have rolled off that couch and done herself a right mischief.'

But Shelley *did* come back. Laura groaned inwardly when she arrived along with Jason, Megan and Oscar again early the following morning. Jason looked tired and his grim expression deepened as the day got busier for his crew. Shelley looked sullen but determined, and totally ignored both Laura and Jean, who were not about to leave her alone with Megan.

Thankfully, she also ignored the baby and, other than disappearing for several hours in the middle of the day, spent her time watching television and reading magazines.

Laura and Tim had an unusually quiet day. The call that came in at four p.m. was only the third one for the shift. An hour later, they had treated a child's asthma attack, transported the young girl to hospital and were returning to the station, planning to give the ambulance a wash down and check equipment stores.

The sight of Mrs McKendry standing at the door of the garage and practically wringing her hands sent a chill snaking down Laura's spine.

'What's wrong? It's not Megan, is it?' The difficulty with which Jean was struggling to find words was unusual enough to hit panic buttons. 'What's happened? Is she—is she all right?'

'We don't know. She's…she's *gone*!'

'Gone where?' Laura's tone sounded curiously blank. Her brain felt foggy, the thought processes slowing enough to make her feel stupid.

'We don't know,' Jean repeated. 'She's just…gone. That *woman* has taken her.' A stifled sob broke through. 'It's all my fault but I had to go and see about the water, didn't I?'

'Where's Jason?'

'They arrived back just a few minutes after I found she'd gone. They've taken the fire engine and the whole crew has gone looking for her. She wouldn't have got far on foot. But…but Jason doesn't know about that *man* yet.'

'What man?'

'The one that left the puir wee bairn on the doorstep in the first place.'

Jason learned about the man soon enough, and Laura heard enough to piece the whole sorry story together as she sat on station in the company of two fire and ambulance crews at shift changeover time.

'It has to be her brother.'

'It was no *brother* that *I* saw that morning. No' the way they were kissing each other.'

'Why didn't you tell us that in the first place, Mackie?'

'Because you wouldn't have taken your wee girl home with you. That Shelley creature is no' fit to be a mother.'

'That was part of the reason I refused to leave Megan at home.' Jason nodded. 'She doesn't know much about babies and she cares even less.' He groaned. 'I had a suspicion she might try and pull a stunt like this. We had an argument last night when her brother was backing her up and trying to intimidate me. They both went oddly quiet when I said we'd have to see what the courts had to say about custody.'

'It's my fault it happened.' If Mrs Mack had been wearing an apron, it would have surprised no one if she'd thrown it over her head.

'You were set up, Mackie. She must have plugged that basin and turned the taps on as soon as she saw Tim and Laura get called out. She had to know you'd go and see what was causing the flood. She was just waiting here long enough for us all to be out at the same time.'

'What are we going to do?' Laura said quietly.

'We didn't see any sign of them on the streets,' Stick said unhappily.

'What did your mate in the police force reckon, Jase?' asked Bruce. 'You did ring him, didn't you?'

Jason nodded wearily. 'He said that it would not be considered kidnapping and if there's no evidence that she's planning to harm the baby then there's absolutely nothing they can do.'

'She's not going to leave town in a hurry.' Stick gave Jason's shoulder a comforting squeeze. 'Let's face it, mate. It's *you* she wants, not the kid.'

'But she can't look after her. She only took her bottle and her blanket. She doesn't even have any clean nappies.'

'She's a woman,' Cliff said somewhat acidly. 'She'll find the shops.'

'She must have looked after her for the first month of her life,' someone from Red Watch added. 'So she must have some idea what she's doing.'

'Ha!' Both Jason and Mrs Mack made identical sounds of contempt.

'She must be staying somewhere.' Laura stood up. 'Let's get the phone book and start ringing motels.'

'And backpackers' hostels,' Jason said. 'Camping grounds, even. You're right, Laura. They're not going to be sleeping on the streets with a baby, even if they don't have much money. We'll find them.'

But they couldn't. They spent hour after hour on the phone until it was so late the responses from motel managers became abusive and Laura finally agreed to go home and get some sleep.

'You've got work starting at seven a.m.'

'So do you.'

'I'll see if I can get someone to cover for me. I need to be around in case Shelley decides to make contact.'

The next day dragged more than any Laura had known. Interest in her patients was at an all-time low and she was very thankful that Tim was prepared to pick up the slack. Between calls, she rang Jason, hoping for news. She found him on station that afternoon, looking bleak.

'I'm not getting anywhere,' he told her wearily. 'Most managers quite rightly refuse to give out any information on their clients.'

'Then let's go and talk to them in person. Even if they won't tell us anything, we can keep our eyes open and even snoop around a bit. We should make a list of all the less expensive places and visit them tomorrow. I'll help as soon as my shift finishes. Are you going home again now?'

'No, I think I'll stay here tonight. She left Megan here the last time she wanted to make a point.'

'She might go back to the house.'

'She didn't last night. I'll go home to get some clothes in the morning and check to see if she's left any kind of message.'

The only message Shelley left was a broken window. Baby equipment and other items were missing but Jason couldn't see any point in reporting the burglary to the police. There was no proof that it had been Shelley and they would be wasting valuable searching time by trying to persuade the authorities to become involved.

Jason and Laura spent the whole of the day visiting the motels in person, trying to persuade people how important it was that they find Megan.

'She's got a medical condition,' Laura invented desperately in the end. 'And her mother hasn't got the medication she needs.'

'Try the police, then. It's none of our business. How do we know you've got any right to be tracking her down, anyway?'

'We could hire a private detective,' Laura suggested late that afternoon. 'They might be better at this than we are.'

'What could they do that we're not doing?'

'I don't know. They might have contacts to track things like credit-card use.'

'She won't need a card for a while,' Jason said. 'She cleaned out my wallet when she broke into the house and I had the rent money for a month in there.'

'She'll be in touch.' Laura was trying to reassure herself as much as Jason. 'As Stick pointed out, it's you she wants. She's just trying to show you that she's capable of taking Megan away. She's betting that you'll be missing her enough to agree to anything to get her back.'

'I *am* missing her. Crazy, isn't it?' Jason pulled Laura into his arms and held her tightly. 'I know you're worried about her just as much as I am but don't worry. We'll get her back...somehow.'

'Are you coming into work tonight?'

'May as well,' Jason said grimly. 'We're not getting anywhere like this so we're going to have to wait for her to contact us. Waiting for that will be a lot easier at work than sitting at home by myself.'

It was a busy night for both the fire and ambulance crews. Laura hardly saw Jason and when they were diverted from returning to station after a job that finished at 6 a.m. she groaned aloud.

'No sleep all night and now a job that will probably make us late and I really wanted to see Jason.'

'Must be tough for you guys at the moment,' Tim said sympathetically. 'Have you got the details for this priority-one through on your pager yet?'

'No. I don't even know what suburb we're supposed to be heading for.' Laura picked up the radio handpiece. 'Inglewood 950 to Control.'

'Must be busy.' Tim noted the length of time taken to respond. 'We'll just keep cruising for a minute.'

'Towards the station,' Laura suggested with a smile. 'That way, if we're too far away from the action they'll have to send someone else.'

'Yeah.' Tim returned the smile but it faded quickly. 'This business with Megan isn't great for you, is it?'

'You could say that.'

'It's funny, but I never thought Jason would be so cut up. He gave the impression that the sooner the mum came back to collect, the better.'

'Things changed,' Laura sighed. 'He fell in love with his baby.'

'And with you?' Tim suggested softly.

'With the whole package,' Laura corrected. 'He doesn't want to lose the family he was given.'

'I can understand that,' Tim said. 'And I can under—'

Whatever else Tim understood was never made clear. The radio crackled into life abruptly.

'Inglewood 950. Priority-one callout. Standby for house fire. Code 61 in attendance.'

Code 61 was the fire service. Maybe Laura would get to see Jason after all. She pushed the button on the side of her microphone.

'Roger. What address?'

Tim had the beacons going. He caught Laura's eye, waiting for the street name. There was no point in picking up speed until they knew they were heading in the right direction.

'Crighton Terrace.' The dispatch officer's tone was perfectly calm. 'No number given.'

Tim's gaze was still on Laura and his eyes widened to reflect her own alarm. He hit the siren and pushed his foot down hard on the accelerator.

Crighton Terrace.

Jason's street. Had Shelley decided to make even more of a point than simply breaking into Jason's house? Was it burning to the ground right now?

And where in God's name was Megan?

CHAPTER TEN

JASON'S house was not on fire.

Laura let out a sigh of relief as they turned into Crighton Terrace. The two fire appliances, beacons lighting up the overcast grey of the dawn sky, were parked at the end of the street beside the old deserted house.

'Probably arson,' she decided aloud. 'No one's lived in that place for months, which would make it a tempting target.'

'Can't see any flames.' Tim sounded vaguely disappointed as he parked well clear of the activity surrounding the fire trucks. 'Bit of smoke, though.'

They skirted a pair of firemen from another station who were unrolling and coupling long lengths of hose. Bruce was standing beside the control panel of the Inglewood appliance. Laura couldn't see Jason anywhere and assumed he must be on the other end of the hose leading through the open front door of the house.

'Anyone injured?' Tim queried.

'Not yet.' Bruce waved towards where their ambulance was parked, its back doors open and the empty stretchers visible. 'Take a pew and put your feet up for a while.'

'Anyone inside the house?'

'Not that we know of. Jase tells us it's been empty for a while. Early morning jogger saw the smoke coming out from under the eaves as he ran past.'

'Can we get a bit closer?' Tim enjoyed watching a different service at work.

'Sure. Just watch you don't trip over any hoses. Or firemen.'

Laura was staring at the house that had become a familiar landmark during her walks with Jason and Megan. She could see fingers of flame reaching out through the smoke billowing out from under the eaves. Only one corner of the house seemed to be involved at present, on both storeys. Her gaze tracked along the side of the house as she wondered where Jason might be.

'Who's upstairs?'

'What?' Bruce had to shout over the sounds of the pump and other fire officers being deployed nearby from the second appliance.

'I saw someone.' Laura pointed. 'At that window.'

'*What?*' Bruce jerked his gaze away from the panel of instruments. 'Are you sure?'

'Yes. Look!' The shape appeared again, a shadowy outline due to the drifts of smoke.

'We haven't got anyone upstairs. The staircase is dodgy.' Bruce was reaching for his radio. 'Jase? Can you hear me?'

A crackling sound came back. 'Affirmative.'

'Looks like there's someone upstairs.'

A swear word came back this time. 'Roger. Send in a ladder. We'll get in at—'

But Laura didn't wait to hear what was planned for the ladder. She had been focussing on another window at the far corner of the house from the flames. She had seen the person again and this time a puff of wind had cleared the drift of smoke for a fraction of a second. Just long enough to recognise the face of the woman. A face framed by long, blonde hair.

'Oh my God!' Laura started running.

'*Laura!*'

The shout from one of the firemen she raced past as they came out of the house sounded like Jason's voice. A heavily gloved hand caught briefly at her arm but Laura was going fast enough to pull away easily.

'Shelley's in there,' she shouted back over her shoulder. 'Megan must be here as well.'

The heat inside the house hit her solidly as she ran through the front door but, surprisingly, the smoke didn't seem too bad. Enough to make her eyes sting and force her to hunch her shoulders and keep her head lowered, but she couldn't see any flames and she knew that the area of the house she had seen Shelley in was as far as it could be from the worst of the fire. If she could just get up the stairs she would be able to find them faster than anybody else because she knew where they were.

She also knew she shouldn't be doing this. She could hear the shouts of the firemen trying to catch up with her. They would pull her clear if they succeeded. Number-one rule for rescuers—do not put yourself in danger. A rule for anyone at a house fire was to get out and stay out. But there was no time to think about anything other than a gut reaction. Laura was running purely on instinct and adrenalin.

This was *Megan* whose life was in danger.

Laura took the stairs two at a time, her eyes now streaming and a painful cough grabbing at her lungs. She heard even louder shouts from the firemen behind her and then she heard something far worse. The crack and rumble of timbers falling as the staircase she had just climbed collapsed.

There was no turning back now and Laura knew she only had a matter of seconds to find what she was looking for. The smoke upstairs was thick. And black. She dropped to her knees to find the only clear patch of air and crawled in a frantic rush towards what she desperately hoped was the room in which she had seen Shelley. God help her if she'd got it wrong!

Everything became a blur. She found the room. Shelley pushed past her at a one-legged crawl, her other leg trailing uselessly behind her. She shouted something at Laura but the words were made incomprehensible by racking coughs. And Laura wasn't listening anyway because it was too hard to think of more than one thing at a time and she could see the small, still shape on the floor beside the window.

It had to be Megan.

The shattering of the window glass was followed by a more ominous sound of something exploding into flames nearby. Laura couldn't breathe any more. Couldn't think. But she didn't need to. Rough, gloved hands were pulling at her, picking her up with Megan still clutched to her. And then she was in Jason's arms.

'Put one arm around my neck. Wrap your legs around my waist and hold on tight!'

If Laura hadn't been so close to losing consciousness or so afraid of whether Megan was still alive or not, she might have been terrified of being carried down the long extension ladder, clinging to the front of Jason's body like a monkey, with Megan wedged securely between them.

Tim came into focus a short time later.

'You bloody idiot,' he told Laura.

She pulled the oxygen mask from her face. 'Wh-where's Megan?' she croaked.

'Right here.'

Laura struggled to sit up. Tim was bent over the second stretcher, with his stethoscope on a tiny chest. Megan's face was covered by the paediatric oxygen mask that was miles too big for her.

'Is...is she...?'

Tim glanced at Laura, then smiled as he lifted the mask from the baby's face for a second. The sound of her crying became separated from the cacophony of shouting, sirens and equipment running outside the ambulance, and Laura laughed and sobbed and coughed all at the same time until Tim gently pushed her back down and firmly tightened the elastic string on her oxygen mask. Laura closed her eyes but not before she caught a glimpse of more ambulance officers rushing past the back doors with another figure on a stretcher.

And then Jason was there. Still in his full protective uniform, he seemed far too large to be standing in the back of an ambulance. His breathing apparatus tank was still on his back, the mask dangling beneath his chin. He ripped off his heavy gloves and his helmet and dropped them onto the floor. Then he reached for Laura's hands.

'You bloody idiot,' he told her. Laura could see tears in his eyes as a wobbly smile appeared. 'Don't you *ever* do that to me again.'

Laura couldn't speak. It was painful to breathe anyway and the look on Jason's face was enough to make her think she *was* precious in her own right. He loved her...there could be no doubt about that. But was it a love that was separate from how he felt about his daughter? Did Jason even know that Megan was all right? Still unable to produce any words, Laura pulled one hand from Jason's grip and pointed to the other stretcher, her lips curving into a smile just as wobbly as Jason's had been.

Jason turned to look at his daughter. The tears that had brightened his eyes overflowed now and built into a trickle that carved a pathway through the grime on his face.

'Thank God,' he whispered. 'I thought that was just *too* much to hope for.'

Had it mattered even more than her well being? 'Sh—' Laura coughed hard and drew in a ragged breath of oxygen. She pulled the mask from her face and tried again. 'Shelley?' she managed to croak.

'Alive,' Jason told her. 'But injured. We got her out just in time. Couldn't do anything to save her brother, or whoever he was, though.'

Whoever he was became clear much later that day.

Laura and Jason found themselves sitting that evening, side by side, on chairs pulled up to a bed in a side room on the orthopaedic ward of Wellington's General Hospital. The woman lying on the bed had her plastered lower leg supported on pillows. Her arms and hands were heavily bandaged and her face was red with areas of peeling skin. With her eyelashes and eyebrows singed to virtual baldness, Shelley Bates looked nothing like the attractive female that had walked into their lives only days before.

The sobbing that had accompanied her confession was only now diminishing, and Laura held tightly onto Jason's hand, unable to swallow the lump in her own throat on witnessing the very real grief on display.

Jason squeezed her hand but his gaze was fixed on Shelley. 'So…if you loved Darryn that much, why were you prepared to marry me?'

'It was Darryn's idea,' Shelley said. 'His best mate—the one in Dunedin—has been living in New Zealand ever since his parents emigrated. Darryn's been wanting to emigrate for years. It was…it was his dream.'

Shelley's voice still sounded hoarse from the damage of smoke inhalation and she coughed at frequent intervals. Laura could sympathise with that discomfort. She also knew that Shelley was far worse off than she was due to the injuries she had received in trying to find and rescue her boyfriend from the fire.

Shelley blew her nose, holding tissues awkwardly between her bandaged hands. 'Is Megan all right?'

'She's fine.' Jason nodded. 'They're keeping her in overnight just to make sure her breathing's not affected.'

'I tried to save her but I couldn't stand up long enough to open the window. I broke my ankle when I fell trying to drag Darryn...and then I *had* to go back for him...'

'She's fine,' Laura said reassuringly. 'You did well, Shelley.'

'No...' Shelley shook her head miserably.

'Yes, you did. If she hadn't been right beside that window it would have been impossible for me to carry her. And putting her on the floor was the best place with all the—'

'No.' Shelley shook her head more vigorously. 'I meant, I'm not Shelley. I'm Sharon.'

'But...' Jason was staring at her blankly. 'The birth certificate says that Shelley is Megan's mother.'

'She is.' The woman in the bed closed her eyes and there was a long silence.

'I don't understand what's going on here,' Jason said finally.

Neither did Laura. 'Are you OK, Shell— Sharon? Do you want me to find a nurse? Do you need to sleep for a while?'

'No.' With a weary sigh she opened her eyes. 'There's no point keeping this up any longer. Not without Darryn.' Tears began to flow again. 'There's no point at all any more.'

'Can you tell us, then?' Jason asked gently. 'Why you've been pretending to be your twin sister?'

'Because Shell always had everything.' Even through her exhaustion and pain, Sharon sounded bitter. 'She was the pretty twin. The clever one. She always got everything she wanted. I was just her shadow. The booby prize.'

'Where is she now?'

'She's dead, like I told you. Except that the blood clot wasn't caused by her being on the Pill. She had to have a Caesarean to have Megan and something went wrong. She did live for a few weeks and she asked me to find you and make sure Megan was going to be all right. She knew I'd never want to bring up her baby and...and that was when Darryn got the idea.'

'Of you marrying me?'

Sharon nodded. 'Shelley said you'd only have to spend some time with Megan to love her and she said you were too nice to abandon your kid after that. I was going to get my permanent residence, divorce you and then find a way to marry Darryn.'

'But that would have taken years.' Laura shook her head.

'That didn't matter. It was Darryn's dream and he's the only person that ever loved me just for myself and not because they couldn't have Shelley.'

Laura felt her level of sympathy rise a few notches. She knew what it was like to want to be loved just for yourself. The plan could have worked, too. Jason would do anything for his daughter now. He probably wouldn't hesitate to marry Laura to give her a mother. In fact, Laura was surprised he hadn't proposed already at some point during the incredibly long day they'd had so far.

'So what now?' Jason asked quietly. 'What do you want us to do, Sharon?'

'I want to go home. As soon as they'll let me. I never wanted to come here at all, really.'

'And Megan?'

'She's your daughter.' Sharon turned her face away. 'That's up to you.'

'We'll do what we can to help you get back to England quickly,' Jason promised her. 'Will you help us sort all the official stuff that will be needed to make sure Megan's allowed to stay with me?'

'Sure.' Sharon's eyes closed again. 'I need to sleep now. Come back tomorrow.'

Hand in hand, Jason and Laura walked through the quiet hospital corridors on their way back to the paediatric ward to see Megan again.

'She's going to be mine,' Jason said in wonder. '*Really* mine.'

'I'm so happy for you, Jase.' It was hard to sound really happy, though, when part of her heart was breaking.

Jason must have caught something in her tone. 'But it means that everything is going to be OK.' Jason pulled Laura to a halt and turned her to face him. 'For *all* of us.' His face lit up as he caught hold of her other hand in his. 'Will you marry me, Laura?' His smile widened. 'And be Megan's *real* mother?'

For a long moment, Laura looked up at Jason, taking in every beloved feature. Then she let her breath out in a soft sigh.

'No,' she said softly. 'I'm not going to marry you, Jason.' Another piece of her heart cracked and she tried to pull her hands free, but Jason's grip was far too strong.

The joy, along with some of the colour, faded from Jason's face. 'But…but why not? I love you, Laura. Megan loves you. I…I thought *you* loved us.'

'I do. And what we have together is wonderful. It's just not enough to base marriage on.'

'But why not?' Jason looked genuinely and totally bewildered. He was still holding Laura's hands as he pulled her gently out of the way of a patient's bed being wheeled along the corridor with attending medical staff. He leaned back against the wall and finally let go of Laura's hands when the procession had passed. 'I don't understand,' he said.

'I'm not going to spend the rest of my life trying to earn your love,' Laura told him gently. 'I've been there and done that and I'm never going to do it again.'

'But I *do* love you.' Jason's voice was loud enough to make one of the nurses following the bed down the corridor to turn and stare. Then she grinned and gave him a thumbs-up signal.

'Not the same way *I* love *you*,' Laura tried to explain. 'And that's what I need if I'm ever going to marry someone and spend the rest of my life with them.'

'But...but I couldn't love you any more than I do.' Jason was trying to keep his voice down but the intensity of his words made it difficult. 'I've finally found out what love really is,' he said. 'I'm *in* love with you, Laura. But I *love* you as well.' He shook his head, frustrated that he couldn't express himself clearly enough. 'I can't lose you,' he added desperately. 'I'll never love anybody the way I love you. You're...you're my *life* now.'

'Not really.' Laura could feel tears gathering as she let Jason's intensity and sincerity wash over her. It was so obviously real. She had known how genuine it was when she'd seen his face in the ambulance that morning. But was that love really for her? The way hers was for him? 'I know you love me, Jase, but how much of how you feel is because I'm part of a package for you?'

'What the hell is that supposed to mean?'

'Megan,' Laura responded simply. 'You want a mother for Megan.'

'*No!*' Jason shook his head sharply. 'Well…yes, but I would want to marry you anyway.'

'Would you?' Laura queried softly. 'Are you sure about that, Jason?'

'Of course I am.'

'When you thought that Shelley—I mean Sharon—was going to take her away, you said yourself that Megan was the most important thing in your life. That *she* was what really mattered.'

'But…' Jason frowned ferociously as he tried to recall the conversation. Then his face cleared. 'Of course I had to do what's best for Megan, but part of why it was so important was to do with you. I knew if I lost her I might lose *you*, and that was a risk I didn't want to take.'

A group of staff heading for supper in the canteen stopped the very private conversation, which was happening in rather a public place, long enough for Jason's words to sink in. Long enough for a bubble of joy to form deep within Laura.

'Why on earth did you think that, Jase?'

'Because she was what brought you into my life. You loved her.'

'But I loved you first.'

'Really?' Jason's smile finally appeared again, just on one side. 'You mean the guys were right? You offered to help me look after Peanut because you fancied me?'

Laura let the embarrassment of having been discussed in such a fashion pass. This was no moment for pride. 'I fancied you the first moment I saw you,' she admitted. 'The first day I started at Inglewood station on Green Watch.' She dipped her head shyly. 'It did take a few weeks to fall in love with you, though.'

'You were *in love* with me? And I didn't know anything about it?'

'Why would you? I didn't really exist as far as you were concerned. Not enough to notice, anyway.'

'I just didn't know you.' Jason looked embarrassed at the truth of Laura's words. 'I was blind, Laura. Immature. Is *that* why you won't marry me?'

'No.'

'Why not, then?'

'Because I can't know whether you love me as much as I love you.'

'I love you more,' Jason declared.

Laura grinned at the confident tone. 'How could you know that?'

'There's more to love. All I have going for me that isn't totally shallow is that I'm Megan's dad.'

'And you thought that would be the reason I'd want to marry you?'

'Why else?'

'Because I *love* you, you bloody idiot,' Laura said through her laughter. 'The way I feel about you has nothing to do with Megan. I'd feel exactly the same if Megan didn't exist.'

'And that's the way I feel about you.'

'Prove it,' Laura challenged.

'OK.' Jason took hold of Laura's shoulders and lowered his head. He kissed her more thoroughly and more tenderly than she'd ever been kissed in her life. A wolf-whistle came from somewhere down the corridor and Jason finally let her go, his expression triumphant. 'How was that?'

'Fabulous.' Laura felt the bubble of joy inside her explode into a tingling excitement that filled every cell in her body.

'So will you believe that I love you...for just you? Will you marry me now?'

'Yes.' Laura laughed. 'I'll marry you, Jase. But I still need more proof.'

'How long will that take?'

Laura's laughter faded until she was simply smiling. 'About a lifetime, I reckon.'

'You're on.' Jason grinned. 'I can manage that, no problem.' He took a confident step forward, tugging on Laura's hand. 'Shall we go and see our baby now?'

'In a minute.' Laura tugged back on Jason's hand and then stood on tiptoe. 'I'd just like a bit more of that proof, first, if you don't mind.'

'Oh, I don't mind a bit,' Jason murmured. His next words were muffled as his lips touched hers. 'We'll take just as long as you need.'

MEDICAL ROMANCE™

Large Print

Titles for the next six months...

August

EMERGENCY AT INGLEWOOD	Alison Roberts
A VERY SPECIAL MIDWIFE	Gill Sanderson
THE GP'S VALENTINE PROPOSAL	Jessica Matthews
THE DOCTORS' BABY BOND	Abigail Gordon

September

HIS LONGED-FOR BABY	Josie Metcalfe
EMERGENCY:	
A MARRIAGE WORTH KEEPING	Carol Marinelli
THE GREEK DOCTOR'S RESCUE	Meredith Webber
THE CONSULTANT'S SECRET SON	Joanna Neil

October

THE DOCTOR'S RESCUE MISSION	Marion Lennox
THE LATIN SURGEON	Laura MacDonald
DR CUSACK'S SECRET SON	Lucy Clark
HER SURGEON BOSS	Abigail Gordon

MILLS & BOON®

Live the emotion

0705 LP 2P P1 Medical

MEDICAL ROMANCE™

Large Print

November

HER EMERGENCY KNIGHT — Alison Roberts
THE DOCTOR'S FIRE RESCUE — Lilian Darcy
A VERY SPECIAL BABY — Margaret Barker
THE CHILDREN'S HEART SURGEON — Meredith Webber

December

THE DOCTOR'S SPECIAL TOUCH — Marion Lennox
CRISIS AT KATOOMBA HOSPITAL — Lucy Clark
THEIR VERY SPECIAL MARRIAGE — Kate Hardy
THE HEART SURGEON'S PROPOSAL — Meredith Webber

January

THE CELEBRITY DOCTOR'S PROPOSAL — Sarah Morgan
UNDERCOVER AT CITY HOSPITAL — Carol Marinelli
A MOTHER FOR HIS FAMILY — Alison Roberts
A SPECIAL KIND OF CARING — Jennifer Taylor

MILLS & BOON®

Live the emotion

0705 LP 2P P2 Medical